TO RAILS UNKNOWN

LUKE BLAKE & TRACEY BLAKE

METAL BRIDGE
PUBLISHING

Published by Metal Bridge Publishing

ISBN: 978-1-7398520-1-6
also available as an e-book

Book design by The Art of Communication
www.book-design.co.uk

Cover design: Ryn Katryn Book Covers
www.rynkatryn.com

About the Authors

Luke Blake has loved stories since he was a young lad. His mother Tracey Blake used to make up stories when walking him to and from School each day, helping him to understand the wide world around him. So it was a natural choice for the two to start collaborating on stories together.

This is their first book that they have worked on together. They hope you enjoy it.

This book is dedicated to my family,
who collectively taught me that different
isn’t wrong.

Luke Blake

To Rails Unknown is a stand alone book that is part of the Schraderverse series.

To Rails Unknown

1

Raising Steam

"Oh perfect, and now it's raining!"

Will was fed up! It was 5pm on a Saturday, it had been a very long day and he was tired. Will was an apprentice engineman on the Great Highland Narrow Gauge Railway, though he lovingly called it the Ginger line as it was much easier to say. Will had planned a lazy evening at home, watching the TV and eating junk food, but his boss had other ideas. There was another apprentice who was training alongside Will. His name was Iain and he was known to hate doing the night shift. The railways staff took it in turns to do the night shifts as few really liked doing them. It was very cold up there at night and the weather could be absolutely awful. However, Will was one of the few who actually enjoyed being on the tracks at night. There weren't any cities or towns along the line, so the sky was very dark. There was no glow of streetlights to hide the beauty of the moon and stars on a clear evening and when he passed the loch, Will always loved to see the reflection of the night sky in the water. It was simply stunning. Also, Will didn't have any family to spend his time with, having lost his parents a few years earlier and, although he had a few friends most of them worked on the railway with him or at the St John's Ambulance station where he was training to be a paramedic in his spare time. So the apprenticeship wasn't only his job, but his social life. Today however, Iain had decided to get a cold and so couldn't manage to work tonight. It was amazing how quickly Iain had been struck down by this cold as he had been fine the day before.

Will's irritation didn't last long though. He had spent the day with his own engine; a beautifully restored Darjeeling 0-4-0 B Class tank engine. When his parents had been killed by a drunk driver, Will had withdrawn into himself and nothing gave him any joy. He had always loved steam engines and his parents had died just after he had started his apprenticeship. One of his friends had heard a rumour about the Darjeeling railway selling off some of its older engines and they were going for a song. This was the catalyst for Will's healing, and he threw himself into buying the B class and arranging for it to be shipped to the UK. He knew that his parents would be over the moon with him spending some of his inheritance on the little engine and that gave him the drive to work through all the red tape involved. Management at the Ginger Line had been amazing. The whole company liked Will and were keen to help him. He had been visiting the line since he was a very small boy and they had watched him grow up so, to see him back to his fun loving, excited self was wonderful for them. After 2 years of struggling and negotiations, the engine, Sherpa, had finally arrived, ready for the long rebuild which took a further 3 years. Sherpa had just completed restoration and passed its boiler safety inspection and was hooked up to a Garratt, ready to formally enter service on the Ginger Line the next day.

The Ginger Line was operational 24 hours a day, 7 days a week which was quite unusual for a narrow-gauge railway, but this particular line connected Knoydart, a very isolated area of Scotland, with the nearest medical facilities in Fort William, a journey of 3 hours, despite only being 46 miles. Only a skeleton staff remained overnight, and tonight Will had been told that he needed to fill in.

The duty manager shouted over "Can you get those wagons ready for tomorrow's 0758, Will?"

"Yep, no worries. I'll do it now." Will brushed his sandy hair out of his blue eyes and headed over to the Indian DM6, a diesel locomotive which was often used to shunt wagons into the right place. He had just pulled up to the engine that was going to be pulling the next day's goods train when an almighty crash roared through the night. Will watched, in horror, as a lorry skidded off the nearby road, down the steep bank of the railway and onto the tracks. Suddenly, there was a huge, ear-ringing explosion and an eye searing ball of fire leapt up into the sky.

For what seemed like an eternity, everything froze. Will was on the ground, having been thrown there by the force of the explosion. He couldn't hear anything, just for a moment and then BANG, his hearing returned and the noise was monumental. People were shouting and screaming, scrambling to try and help the driver of the lorry and to save the precious equipment that the railway had stored at that part of the depot. Will struggled to his feet and headed for a hose pipe. He knew that he had to keep those flames at bay until the fire brigade could arrive.

"Good lad, Will. Are you OK? Not hurt?" It was the

duty manager, Stan.

"Just bumps and scrapes I think. Nothing serious. Is everyone else OK?"

"All accounted for. No injuries thank goodness." Stan's reply was calm and reassuring. It was as if he was talking about his next meal rather than dealing with an explosion. But Stan had been a military man. He knew how to deal with an emergency and once he knew his team was safe, he was able to move on to the next task.

"You keep that hose on the fire. I have called the brigade, they are on their way but it could take them a while to get here. It's a long way from town."

Will did his best, but the fire was spreading too quickly. The other staff members who were on duty started trying to damp down the flames too, but it was no good. The fire was spreading and getting dangerously close to the fuel tanks which were full of diesel for the engines.

One of the locos in the siding by Will was a huge South African NGGI6 Beyer Garratt, which was coupled up to two other engines, one of which was Will's own Darjeeling, and the other the railway's oldest engine which was a Stainz class 0-4-0 tank engine which was simply called Number 4. It was a piece of history as it was built in 1889.

"We can't lose those engines" Will shouted, as he gave his hose pipe to one of the workers from the nearby farm who had headed down to see if they could help. He charged over to the stranded engines, jumping over debris as he went.

"Will. Stay where you are. We can't save them all," Stan bellowed at him.

Will ignored him. He was not going to lose his beloved Darjeeling.

Will leapt into the cab of the Garratt and threw the reverser to full forward and released the brakes. Then he opened the regulator and steam had just started to fill the cylinders when disaster struck. The fire reached the fuel tanks and an almighty fire ball engulfed the stricken lorry. The lorry exploded with an eerie blue glow which engulfed Will and his line of engines.

When the dust and smoke settled, and that blue glow had diminished, Will and his train were nowhere to be seen. Three steam engines had, inexplicably, disappeared.

2

Onto Unknown Rails

"Ooooowwwwww, my head!!!!" Will groaned as he woke up. There was a nagging throb in the back of his head which was only made worse when he sat up. It took a moment for Will to recall what had just happened. He struggled to his feet and took a deep breath. There was the usual smell of an in-steam locomotive which was comforting but he dreaded looking out of the cab and seeing a scene of utter destruction that must have been the result of that explosion. Will had never experienced anything like it before and he hoped never to again. His body screamed protest at him as he leant on the side of the cab, trying to get his bearings.

Will was stunned by what he saw. Will peered out of the engine to a scene of utter tranquillity. He couldn't believe that he had been unconscious long enough to miss the fire brigade coming to the aid of the railway. He was also a little disappointed that he had been left on the engine for so long but assumed that everyone had been busy with the aftermath of the explosion.

It was quiet now, other than the sound of steam hissing through the pipes. All Will could hear were the normal sounds of the countryside; birds, trees blowing in the breeze and the sound of water lapping on the shore.

"Hang on! Water, on the shore? There isn't any water in the train yard! What is going on," he wondered aloud.

This was certainly not the train yard he had left, what felt like moments ago.

The engines were still on a railway line, although it was a different line to the one Will usually travelled along. Will jumped out of the cab and had a look around. The land was gently sloping upwards on either side and the slopes were covered in long grass which seemed greener than any along the Ginger Line. Just back from the line were a row of huge trees, which seemed to have a purplish fruit hanging from the branches. Will wasn't much of a forager, but he was sure that he had never seen fruit like it. It looked like an apple, but bigger and growing in bunches. Other than that, there wasn't much to see. Will felt that he should get out of the hills so he could take a look around and find out where he was. Then he could just head back to the station and see what had happened after that explosion. So, he climbed into the cab and started the engine moving slowly forward. As he went, he could feel the hairs on the back of his neck sticking up. He felt a shiver go down his spine and was sure that someone, or something, was watching him!

At the top of the rise on the left side of the train, in one of the marla trees, sat a small creature. He hid behind the leaves and branches of the marla tree and stared, in wonder, at the line of steaming metal dragons moving slowly along the metal line. Once the coast was clear, the creature slipped from his hiding place and raced through the grass. He knew he had to get to Nirvana, the leader of the kitsune, and tell her what he had found. She would know what to do.

Meanwhile, on the train, Will was getting more and more concerned with each mile he travelled. He knew, without a shadow of a doubt, that he was not on the Ginger Line anymore. Will knew every turn and siding of that line and none of the rails he was on were familiar. He tried the radio to see if he could get some help, but there was no response. Just static! All he could do was keep creeping forward and look for any signs of civilisation. After all, these tracks had to lead somewhere, didn't they? Night began to fall and it got really dark outside. The engine's headlights were on, and they lit up the space in front of him, but Will was still feeling uneasy. Suddenly, he saw movement off to the side of the track. Will stopped the train and peered out of the cab. He couldn't hear much over the noise of the engine, but what he could hear was terrifying. It sounds like a battle scene from a film. Then, on top of all the noise, Will saw lights flashing in the sky.

"What is going on? I guess I am going to have to take a look. Stay here."

Will stopped, and laughed at himself, realising that he had just told his engines to stay on the line! Thinking that he must be going crazy, Will turned on the torch on his mobile phone and picked his way along the line to see what was creating all the noise and light. What he found was completely astonishing.

Knights! Knights in armour, like something out of a story about King Arthur and his Round Table. But these knights were attacking unarmed creatures and that didn't seem to be knightly behaviour as far as Will was concerned! Then Will realised that some of the creatures, who genuinely looked a bit like foxes, were a lot smaller than the others. Children. They had children with them. Those children were being protected by one foxy lady whilst the others were trying to keep the knights at bay.

Assuming he had come across some kind of theatrical production, Will began to approach one of the costumed characters to ask where he was when suddenly, one of the fox-creatures fell at his feet, with a gaping wound across his chest. Will couldn't get over how realistic the wound was and bent down to inspect it.

That was the moment when he realised that this wasn't a play at all. The wound was real as were the fox-creatures and Will had never seen anything like them before. He also realised that the knights were actually trying to kill these fox-creatures.

Will only had a moment to be astonished by this revelation before realising that he had to do something. He couldn't let those children be hurt. Thinking swiftly, he assumed that, as the knights seemed to be wearing medieval style armour, they may not have seen anything like his locomotives before. He charged back to the Garratt and got it going again, driving it straight towards the scene of the battle. He put the headlights on to full and lit up the clearing, he blew his whistle and, after bringing the engine to a halt in between the two groups, opened the regulator making steam shoot out from the open cylinders. Everything stopped. Will took the opportunity to inform the knights that their behaviour left a lot to be desired and that they should vacate the area. For good measure he impressed upon them how undignified they would look if the engine rolled over them and dented their beautiful, shiny armour. For a moment, nobody moved a muscle and then the Knights decided that they weren't dressed for the occasion and turned and fled. Not the other creatures though. They stayed right where they were, staring at the metal monsters in front of them and then at Will, who smiled back reassuringly. After what seemed like an age, one of the smaller creatures slipped past the foxy lady guard and crept up to the front of the Garratt. He reached out a hand and tentatively touched the engines front coupler, then snatched his hand back again. All the creatures acted as one and raced towards the child. He wasn't hurt though, just scared. Will knew he had to go and meet these fox-like creatures and so, once again, stepped out of the cab of his engine and moved into the beam of the head lights.

"He is human," someone gasped.

"A human helped us?" another replied.

There was a hum of excited conversation as the fox creatures discussed this detail, but Will had seen that some of the creatures were hurt. He reached back into the cab and grabbed the first aid kit. He carefully approached one of the creatures and pointed to a nasty wound on his arm.

"Can I help you with that?" Will asked and he opened the kit to show the man what was inside.

The creature thought for a moment, looking Will straight in the eyes and then nodded and sat on the ground.

"This might hurt a bit," Will told him. "But it will clean the wound and make sure it isn't infected."

"I understand. You may proceed."

Gradually, Will treated the wounds of this creature and many of the others. He learned that they were called kitsune and that they had a village not far from the clearing that they were in.

Will had just finished cleaning another cut when a commotion at the other side of the clearing caught his attention. Another group of kitsune, this time more heavily armed, appeared out of the trees. Seeing Will, they assumed that he was an enemy and moved towards him aggressively. Quickly, the kitsune that Will had rescued surrounded him and started speaking to the newcomers, reassuring them that Will was not an enemy and that he had, in fact, rescued them from King Starin's men. The newcomers were still scowling and glaring at Will, but they agreed that the best thing to do was to head to the city and let Nirvana decide what to do with him.

The head newcomer instructed Will to start up his engine again.

"These metal lines come into the city, and you can save the injured a long walk."

As Will and the kitsune headed to the city, the soldiers Will had scared off arrived at their headquarters to report to their leader, King Starin.

King Starin was not the kind of leader who took failure well. After brutally questioning the soldiers, he had them sent to the dungeons to be tortured. He then called his advisors to him and ordered that Project Downfall was to proceed at full speed.

3

A New Shed to Call Home

Will and the kitsune leaders managed to squeeze everyone from the clearing onto the train and set off for the city. The atmosphere wasn't exactly friendly and Will wondered what he had got himself into! Hoping to ease tensions, Will tried to start a conversation with the head newcomer.

"What is the name of the city we are heading for?"

No reply.

"OK! What is your name then?"

"Be silent, Human. We aren't your friends!!!"

"Alrighty then. I'll just drive the train. To the city with no name."

Will heard a little giggle off to his left and turned his head slightly. One of the kitsune children was hiding behind her hand, so Will gave her a grin and a wink. She blushed bright red and turned into the arms of the foxy lady who had been protecting the children in the clearing. Will turned his grin on her and received an icy glare in return. He sighed and continued monitoring the engine's dials.

Finally, after what seemed like an age, Will was told to stop. A kitsune leapt from the engine to stand in front of it, between the rails. He lifted his arms and gave a short incantation of some sort. To his utter astonishment, Will watched a gateway just appear, out of thin air, right in front of the train.

"Don't just stand there gawping, go through," one of the kitsune commanded.

Will did as he was ordered and slowly drove his procession of engines through the gateway and into an enormous, makeshift city.

As with most cities, there was a buzz of activity and noise and all around him, people were going about their business. However, the people in this city were unlike any that Will had ever seen before. Even the term "people" seemed wrong. It was as if he was looking at the glossary of a Grimms Fairy Tale . There were creatures of all kinds; faeries, lizard people, elves, dwarves and countless others that Will could not even name.

"Stop!" a voice commanded. Will did as he was ordered and shut the engine down.

"I can't just switch it off. I have to dump the fire or the water will evaporate and the boiler will explode," Will had explained. After some muttered conversations a runner headed off into the darkness. Shortly afterwards four lizard-like creatures came running towards the engines. They were carrying some kind of metal box which they quickly slipped under the engine. Will realised that they wanted him to dump the fire into this box so he directed them to place it in exactly the right place, before pulling the lever which opened the bottom of the fire box. Once the fire had been dumped, Will could safely shut the engine down.

With a warning to the crowds to not touch the engine as it was still hot, Will was taken to a grassy area where a crowd of kitsune were waiting. Off to one side there was a log cabin. It was a big cabin, but nothing fancy. The roof was made of grass turfs which were covered in wildflowers. If Will hadn't been trying to hide the fact that he was terrified at that moment, he might have stopped to admire the building. It truly was beautiful.

The lead kitsune grabbed Will's arm and dragged him into the cabin. Inside, he could see a circular table, surrounded by wooden chairs. Most of the chairs were occupied by a being of some description. There were 10 chairs in total and 8 of them were filled. At the far end of the table stood a kitsune woman who could only be described as imposing. She had long black hair and a stern face, with a long nose and piercing eyes which were such a dark brown that they almost appeared to be black. Her 9 tails were spread out behind her in a fan arcing up her back, their white tips crowning her head. She was dressed in the same, plain clothing, as the other city dwellers with nothing defining her as the leader. But Will was in absolutely no doubt that she was in charge! She had an aura of command about her, the likes of which Will had never experienced before. And she was glaring at him!

"My name is Nirvana and I lead the Folk of Vitea. Who are you and what are you doing in our lands?"

Nirvana's voice was cold as steel. A shiver went down Will's spine and he had to give himself a good shake in order to reply to her questions. "C'mon Will Lad, put your Big Boy Pants on. You've done nothing wrong," he told himself.

"My name is Will Thorpe. I was in an accident on the railway line and when I woke up, I was here. I don't know where 'here' is and I don't know whose lands I am in."

"A likely story, Human. You are one of Starin's scum, aren't you? You positioned yourself in the woods so that my people would find you, didn't you. You are here to spy on us and our capabilities. Well, you won't be returning to him with any information!" Nirvana turned away from Will and addressed those sat at the table. "What say you?" she asked of them.

Each and every one of the creatures at the table turned their eyes to look at Will and then back at their leader.

As one, they said "Execution!"

Will's legs almost turned to water. He could not believe what he had just heard and found himself thinking that it was true what they say about no good deed goes unpunished.

The lead kitsune from the clearing marched smartly over to Will and drew the long-bladed knife that was strapped to his belt. He moved behind Will and kicked him in the back of the knees. Once Will was kneeling on the floor, the kitsune dragged his head back by the hair and exposed his neck, ready for the killing blow. He looked to his leader, awaiting her final confirmation.

Suddenly, the door to the cabin flew open and banged against the wall. The kitsune with the knife threw Will to the floor, where he lay gasping, and sprang to the side of his leader, ready to defend her life. It all happened in a split second, but to Will it felt like slow motion. At the door stood the foxy lady from the clearing. She was panting with exertion and her ears were pressed flat against her head, in anger.

"Hold!" she screamed. "You cannot do this."

"Rosa, what is the meaning of this?" Nirvana demanded. "How dare you barge in late like that. We are in the middle of a legal hearing."

"Mother, you call this a hearing? Was the prisoner allowed to defend himself? Was he allowed to do more than just tell you his name? I doubt it! He saved us? He frightened off Starin's soldiers and he helped the injured. He brought us back to the city, to safety, and you decide to execute him? It's wrong and you know it Mother. Have you seen the machines he has? Can you imagine how powerful they could be in this battle? They could give us a massive edge over Starin and his troops."

Will could do nothing but stare at the Foxy Lady, Rosa. She looked a lot like Nirvana with her long black hair and pointed ears sticking out of the top of her head. Those ears were constantly in motion, expressing the emotions that were also plain on Rosa's face. Her green eyes flashed in her oval face and her perfect skin was tinged red, with anger. Her tails started out as a fan, like her mother's but as she spoke, her tail moved and gathered together. It swished from left to right, like that of an angry cat. She was mesmerising and Will couldn't stop himself from looking at her in wonder.

Over the next hour, Rosa managed to convince the council that Will should be kept alive and that his machines should be put to good use; helping them in the fight against Starin, whoever he was! The council did set certain conditions when agreeing to keep Will alive. He could have unlimited access to the engines so they would be ready to use at short notice, but he was to be under guard at all times. The only other time that he would be allowed out in the City of Hope was to get meals. Will wasn't concerned about these rules. If he had his engines, food and a place to sleep he was happy. The same could not be said for Rosa though. She was fuming!!! Her mother had assigned her as Will's personal guard and she hated guard duty. All that sitting around, confined to the city was her idea of hell and it showed on her face. Will was a little scared as he left the council meeting!

Rosa led Will to a hut off to the side of the clearing. "This is where I live" she told him "which means it's where you live now, too. Don't make a mess or I will beat you" Rosa's tail was still bristling and her ears were pressed down against her skull so Will was fairly certain that she meant every word she said!

"Ok," he quavered.

Suddenly, there was a loud knocking at the door of the hut. "Rossssa, are you there?"

Rosa stalked over to the door and threw it open to admit, what Will could only describe as, a lizard on 2 legs and looked like a humanised Godzilla. He had dark green, scaly skin which shone in the sunlight. His mouth was filled with pointed, bright white teeth and his tongue often popped out between them.

Really. That's what he looked like!

"So'Ren, am I pleased to see you. Mother made me the humans guard so I have to stay with him at all times. The alternative was to have him executed and his machines destroyed, and I couldn't let her do that."

Rosa spun round to face Will, her teeth bared, and her tails gathered into a tight rope. "Know this HUMAN! My debt to you is paid. You rescued us and I returned the favour. But I don't trust you and I will be watching your every move."

Will was taken aback by the fury in Rosa's eyes. They looked like two crystals glinting in the dim light of the hut. He swallowed hard and nodded at her. He was fairly sure that her anger was actually at the fact that she had to act as his guard/babysitter, rather than at him. But he wasn't certain.

"I understand. Thank you. But why do you hate humans so much? What have they done to you that could make you feel this way?"

"What have you done? Why are we so angry? Are you joking?" Rosa was so mad that she was actually spluttering. All of a sudden, sparks started flying from her fingers and a green glow surrounded her. Will was terrified, and fascinated at the same time. Now, she was angry at him.

"Rossssa, ssstop. You will burn the city to the ground at thissss rate. Could it be that he really doesss not know? Where are you from, human?"

For a moment Will wasn't able to answer. Between Rosa's fury and So'Ren's hypnotising voice, he was a little overwhelmed. But, after a moment he realised that the lizard like man was talking to him.

"Sorry, what? Where am I from? I live in Scotland but I am originally from Carlisle. And my name is Will, not Human."

"I apologise Will. I have never heard of those places. Are they near here? I thought I knew all of the villages on Vitae."

"Vitae? What is Vitae?" Will asked.

Rosa and So'Ren looked at each other in amazement. Then So'Ren replied "Vitae is here. The planet we live on. Our home."

4

MAKING NEW FRIENDS

Over the next few days, Rosa and So'Ren told Will all about their home. At first, they didn't believe that he was actually from another world, but as they got to know him, they realised that he was telling them the truth.

"So, the king is called Starin, but he isn't your king? "

So'Ren muttered something under his breath that Will didn't quite catch.

"Language!" Rosa laughed. "You are right of course. Just don't let your parents hear you saying that word! If I wasn't afraid of my mother I might have used a stronger word" she laughed again.

Will loved watching Rosa and So'Ren exchanging banter in this way but it made him feel a bit lonely. Not that he had any family back on Earth, but he missed his friends on the Ginger Line. Being part of a community was a great feeling and he wondered if he would ever feel that way again. Sadly, whilst Rosa and So'Ren were warming up to Will, the other residents of the City of Hope did not feel the same way. Whenever they went out into the city an extra guard had to join them. This was after their first venture to see the sights, which had taken them to a beautiful building which was used as a sanctuary and place of peace, where folk could talk to their spirit guides and past masters. The building was set slightly apart from the main residential area of the city. It was on a small rise and surrounded by lush gardens which were obviously very well looked after. A stream flowed alongside the building and the sound of the rushing water added to the feeling of calm that washed over Will as he approached. Inside the sanctuary there were shelves and alcoves which displayed pieces of artwork and ancient books. Will was stunned at the workmanship of the artefacts. The colours were so vivid and bright. There was such an air of optimism about most of the pieces. There were paintings which depicted scenes of tranquillity and gratitude, pottery with glorious beings carved into them and so many other pieces that Will knew he would have to visit the sanctuary many more times to see it all.

When Rosa finally led them back out into the sunshine, they had been confronted by an angry crowd, furious that Will had desecrated their sanctuary. Rocks and punches were thrown and only Rosa's presence stopped the situation from escalating further. Although he wasn't badly hurt, the bruises reminded Will of how precarious his situation was and of how much danger he was in.

The following morning, Rosa and Will were sat on the ground outside her hut. Rosa did a morning exercise routine which resembled the yoga classes he had seen at the gym at home. As he was very bored and going a bit stir crazy from being cooped up for so long, Will had started copying her moves and joining in with her. At first, she had laughed at his clumsy efforts but after a couple of days she had started encouraging him and correcting his stances. Will couldn't believe how hard he was having to work and how tired his body was after one of these sessions. But man it felt good!

One morning, they were sitting in the grass, drinking a cup of tea (of sorts) and just watching the world go by. So'Ren had joined them, and they were chatting away when a loud ringing sound started echoing around the city. It was coming from the huge gates and Will could see that they were just swinging open.

"Make way. We have wounded. Get the medica," a voice bellowed. The voice belonged to a huge bear of a man who was leading the incoming group into the city. Behind him came a ragtag group of creatures; some carrying stretchers, others clearly injured. Will had run forward to try and give aid. At first his efforts had been pushed away, but Will was having none of that. His paramedic training kicked in and he was able to switch off all other distractions and just focus on what needed doing. At first he had helped carry stretchers, but then he realised that he was wasting his knowledge so he chose an injured elven woman from the crowd and took in her injuries. Her left arm hung at a strange angle and the pain of it showed clearly on her pale, blood streaked face.

"Here, let me help," Will offered.

"Don't touch me, human," she yelled back at him.

"OK, but if your shoulder stays like that much longer, your arm will never work properly again."

The woman looked over at the medicas for help, but they were all busy helping the worst of the injured folk. She desperately looked around for someone else to help her, but Will was the only one available.

"Alright human. But I am armed."

Will couldn't help himself and started laughing at the elven woman's unintentional pun. After a moment she realised what she had said and smirked.

"Oh ha ha. Now get on with it," she snapped.

"Alright, alright. Don't worry. I am armless!"

With the tension broken, Will was able to make the woman comfortable and she, in turn, helped him to work with other injured folk.

Will cleaned and bandaged wounds and helped splint broken bones. Rosa was stunned by his actions and ultimately, this was the reason that she had decided to fully trust him.

Rosa and So'Ren told Will how Starin's family had always hated the magical community. It was believed that the hatred came from jealousy over not having any magic themselves. Humans seemed to feel that if they didn't have magic, then no-one should have it. Things had always been difficult between humans and magical creatures, but Starin had taken things to a whole new level. He had developed machines that could kill and injure thousands of creatures at one time, and he had started using them more and more frequently. He had been king for 15 years and in that time had killed more magical creatures than all of his family before him.

Will was taken to where the dead were remembered by their loved ones. It wasn't a graveyard, but rather a garden of memory. A flower, which looked like a white rose and was called a Spiritaeus, was planted for every person who had died, and the garden was covered in them. There was almost no space left. Row upon row of flowers were laid out before him and, for a moment, Will was too stunned to speak. He had never understood hatred of any kind and this beautiful display was almost more than he could take. Rosa took him along one of the rows and sat down about halfway along it.

"This is my father's Spiritaeus. He was killed, many years ago, in an attack by Starin's army. He was a wonderful father and my mother adored him. She was never the same after his death, becoming a driven woman. Everything she did, and still does, was aimed at destroying Starin and his generals in the palace. My fathers death was one of thousands. Humans have almost destroyed the folk and that is why you have been treated so badly. It is why we could…should, never be friends," Rosa explained, sadly. She turned and looked Will in the eyes and he saw that hers were full of unspilled tears.

Will reached out and took Rosa's hand, gave it a quick squeeze and then released it. He stood and walked amongst the Spiritaeus, reading the little name plaques and growing ever more despondent at the actions of the humans on this world. Never before had Will felt such shame. The death of so many of the folk was not on his hands, but knowing that his race had committed these atrocities was almost more than he could bear.

Once he had collected himself, Rosa and Will left the garden. They were joined by So'Ren and the three of them headed to the infirmary, where the medicas were treating the wounded and sick. Will had wanted to stay and help but he had been asked to leave after a while. He did not know the biology of most of these creatures and was little more than a distraction.

Will found himself wondering what kind of culture would want to wipe out another just for being different. Then he thought about the wars on his own planet and how they had started. It seemed to him that, wherever humans went, they caused destruction and pain.

Seeing his distress, Rosa took Will to his engines. She knew that they would make him feel better and, she was right. As Will ran his hands over the Darjeeling engine, he began to calm down. He was not responsible for his whole race; he could only be the best person he knew how to be and hope that was enough. With that thought firmly in his mind, Will started to do his daily checks on the engines. So'Ren was in his usual place, looking over Will's shoulder. The lizard man had turned out to be a genius engineer. He had asked Will to explain his engines and had intuitively understood what each component did and what it was responsible for. So'Ren had even started showing up each day with pieces of expertly crafted metal which were perfectly formed to fit onto Will's Darjeeling engine. Whilst the engine was in good shape, So'Ren was able to see where a minor adjustment could improve the engines performance. The two of them had had some very technical conversations about what the engine needed and how it was powered. So'Ren had some fantastic ideas for replacing the coal that the Darjeeling used as its power source.

"We have infernoss crystalss, which power everything that needss a large energy ssource. We could adapt your Darjeeling to use the infernoss crystalss in place of that dirty coal."

"Really? You can do that? " Will asked.

"Of coursse! It won't be eassy, but I ssee no reasson that it can't be done! It will take time though."

When Will and So'Ren got started on this type of conversation, Rosa would wander away from them and practise her sword work. Of course, watching Rosa work out was a sure-fire way of getting Will to stop talking about trains! She moved like a dancer and Will was mesmerised by her. This was a bit of a problem though as Rosa could sense Will's attention and she loved to tease Will about it.

"Will you stop staring at my rump!" she shouted as she spun around, glaring at him.

"What? Rump? What? Errr. Train. Err what were you saying So'Rump Ren! So'Ren! What's that over there? Owww!" Will had walked into the Garratt in his haste to get away from Rosa's glare. He turned around to see Rosa and So'Ren holding their sides and laughing out loud.

"Awwwww Will. I have never seen anyone blush sso prettily!" So'Ren laughed.

Will heaved a great sigh and headed off to the other side of the engine to continue his work.

Later, that evening, Will was just finishing up when he rounded the Darjeeling and saw Nirvana examining the engine. Now, Will had retained a healthy wariness of the kitsune commander. She had, after all, decided to execute him in the past! So he was a little nervous of approaching her. But, with his big boy pants firmly pulled up, he headed over to where Nirvana stood.

"Good evening, Nirvana. How are you today? Is there something I can help you with?"

At first, Nirvana did not reply. She continued to stare at the Darjeeling's dirty blue paint. But after a moment she turned her obsidian eyes to Will and sighed.

"I am aware of the time you have spent in the infirmary and in our garden of remembrance."

"Oh, err, yes. I hope that is alright. I didn't mean to cause any offence," Will stammered in reply.

"No offence was taken, and you are free to visit these places, as long as my daughter is with you. But, I am curious as to why you visited these places? My medicas tell me that you are keen to help and, once you have learned about the folk of Vitae, you will be an asset to them, but humans don't heal the fae; they kill them. So can you see why I am confused?"

"I do see, and I don't have a good answer. I can only say that, on my planet, not all humans are evil. There have been evil people, but there have been more good people. And, ultimately, I think good usually wins out. I don't know much about Vitae, or your history, but what I do know is that all folk should be treated as equals, no matter the colour of their skin, their beliefs or their way of life. If everyone respected the folk around them, the world would be a better place. I bet most of the humans on this planet have more in common with you than you think. I know you don't want to hear that but, when I look at the history of my planet, a lot of humans were forced into doing bad things or lied to by their leaders. Or the hatred had gone on for so many years, they just didn't know any better." Will stopped talking. He could see that Nirvana didn't want to hear good things about humans, but something in his last sentence seemed to be occupying her thoughts. So, he let the silence continue for a while.

"The violence against the folk has been going on for a long time," she finally said. "Starin, didn't start it. He is just the last in a long line of humans who want to destroy us. But, as you say, we also want to destroy the humans, so does that make us as bad as them? I need to think more on this. We are having a council meeting tomorrow. I would like you to come to it. Will you do that?"

"Well. I guess that depends on whether you are going to try and execute me again!" Will replied in a light-hearted way. He grinned at Nirvana and, after a moment, she returned a smile.

"No promises," Nirvana quipped. "But please, come anyway."

The next morning, Will and Rosa headed over to the council meeting once more. Will had to admit that he was a little nervous. He wondered what Nirvana had up her sleeves and why she had personally asked him to attend the meeting. Rosa wasn't much help. She either didn't know or just wasn't saying, what Nirvan had planned. But, she didn't seem any more irritated than usual so maybe that was a good sign.

As they entered the chamber, the hubbub of noise suddenly ceased. All eyes turned to look at Will.

NWith the grace of a hunter, Nirvana glided over to Will's side.

"Welcome Will. Thank you for coming to this meeting." Nirvana smiled at him and winked.

Rosa's face was a picture! She seemed amazed that her, usually cold and distant, mother was smiling at this human. But, Will had grown on Rosa too. He just seemed to charm everyone he met with his easy humour and kind heart. He was handsome too, Rosa thought. For a human, obviously. Rosa's thoughts were interrupted as her mother began to speak again.

Nirvana went to stand at the head of the council table and addressed those present in her commanding voice.

"I invited Will to this meeting today as I have been watching him during the time he has spent with us. I have seen nothing but good in him, and we have had a very interesting conversations! I believe my hasty judgement of him was in error. In fact, I now believe that Will should be allowed to become one of the Folk of Vitae, and be allowed freedom within our walls. What say you?"

SILENCE

Nobody said anything. For what seemed like an eternity, every member of the council just sat staring at Nirvana as if she had grown an extra pair of ears.

"What say you?" Nirvana repeated.

Then the noise started. There was uproar. Every council member was shouting to try and be heard over the noise of the others. Eventually Rosa shouted for quiet and order was restored.

"I have spent every day with Will and agree that he has a good heart and that he will act in the interest of this community. He is a little irritating, but I am sure that we can beat that out of him, over time. My vote is for inclusion into the Folk of Vitae."

Nirvana, Rosa and Will turned their attention to the folk sat at the table. Nirvana and Rosa seemed to be daring anyone at the table to disagree with them. Will knew that, if he was going to be accepted, he would need to win these people around.

"May I say something?" he asked.

All eyes in the room turned to him. Nirvana nodded and Will had to take a deep breath before he could continue.

"I know that you have been mistreated by humans. I know, and understand, why you hate us so much. I am sorry for the pain and suffering you have experienced at the hands of King Starin's kind. I would like to tell you that the humans on my world are different, but I can't. All I can say is that there are more good than bad and I would like to believe I am one of the good ones. I can only promise you that I will never treat you in the way other humans have treated you. I will fight alongside you to defeat Starin and to end his tyranny. You deserve to be free and I will do everything in my power to help you achieve that.

There are some of you who may wish to take advantage of my engines, but I don't want you to allow me to join you for that reason. I want you to allow me to join you because we have similar goals; to rid this world of Starin and to gain freedom for the Folk of Vitae.

Nirvana, with your permission, I will leave this council for now. I know you have much to discuss."

Once again there was silence as Will waited for Nirvana to allow him to leave. Then, before she could answer, a murmur started to pass around the room. Council members were whispering to each other, discussing what Will had said.

Nirvana glanced at Will and gave a slow, deliberate wink. Unsure what she meant by it, Will remained standing in front of the table. Finally, one of the council members stood. He was a curious mix of human and eagle; called a harpy. His name was Stormwind and he had the power to create gusts of wind so strong that they could knock over pretty much anything in his path. That included carts and buildings. Rosa had described him as full of hot air, but a decent sort. He was the master of spies and probably knew more about Starin and his forces than any other of the Folk of Vitae.

"Human..."

"My name is Will."

Stormwind looked a bit taken aback by Will's interruption at first, but then nodded his head in acquiescence.

"My apologies. Will. I, like my fellow council members, have my concerns about admitting a human into our midst. But. Your words moved me. It could be said that not all folk of Vitae are good. We have some bad apples here too."

Will thought Stormwind's eyes looked over to another of the council members, but he couldn't be sure. He made a mental note to ask Rosa about it later. Stormwind continued, "I also know that there are good people amongst the humans too. Starin rules by fear and many have no choice but to serve him, lest their families be slaughtered."

After this comment there was uproar! Council Members were shouting over each other, fists were being shaken and tempers were being thoroughly lost. The loudest, shrillest voice belonged to Veneema, a female naga. She was part humanoid, part snake, with her lower body being a snake's tail. She had venomous fangs and was covered in scars. She looked like she had been in a battle or two. Veneema and Stormwind stood face to face, bellowing at each other. No need to ask Rosa who Stormwind's enemy was now, thought Will!

Rosa had warned Will that Veneema was a troublemaker and hated all humans with a passion. She had been captured by them as a young naga and had been tortured and left for dead. However, nagas are not so easy to kill. She had managed to escape from Starin's dungeons and make her way back to the City of Hope but had never fully recovered from the horrors she had experienced. Now, filled with hate, she was the council member who most strongly supported war with Starin. She wanted to obliterate all humankind, but not before she had made them suffer. Her fangs were never empty of poison!

After what seemed an age, Nirvana called for quiet. Such was the power of her presence, she only needed to call for it once and all of the council were back in their places, looking at her expectantly.

"You have heard Will's words. You know my thoughts. You need to decide, here and now. Do we admit Will to the Folk of Vitae? What say you?"

Nirvana looked at each council member in turn and they indicated their decision with either a nod or a shake of their head. Rosa noted down their responses. There were 10 Council Members in all, not including Nirvana. She had the deciding vote in the event it was needed. Of the 10, 9 nodded. Only Veneema shook her head.

Will let out a sigh of relief and he was duly admitted to the Folk of Vitae. No ceremony, no fuss. Just accepted into the fold.

That's exactly how I like it, Will told himself.

The council meeting was just drawing to its close when the sound of running feet caused a hush to fall over the room. A lizard creature came charging into the chambers, panting and gasping as he came. He was one of the roving scouts who patrolled outside of Vitae, gathering information and relaying it, one scout to the next, back to the council.

"King Ssstarin's forces are advancing on Sssea Town. Their defences will never hold. We have to help them!!!"

Nirvana approached the scout.

"When did this happen?"

"Thisss morning. Jusst after firsst light."

"You have done well to get this to us so quickly. Thank you. There is little we can do to help the citizens of Sea Town as it will take at least 6 days to get our forces there in enough numbers to force Starin's troops back. All we can do is try and rescue any of the folk who make it out," Nirvana stated calmly. This was not the first time she had to make such a difficult announcement. As she looked around the council members she noticed Will frowning and shaking his head.

"Will? You have something to say? "

"Are there any cart tracks to Sea Town," Will asked?

"Yes, of course. It is where we get most of our imports of fish from." Nirvana replied.

"Well, why don't we let the train take the strain?" Will laughed. At the confused looks from the folk around him he continued, "my engines can get us there much more quickly. We may be able to do more than just pick up refugees. We may be able to evacuate the whole town."

Council members immediately started discussing this with each other and the noise level in the chambers started to rise again. Nirvana quickly spoke above the hubbub.

"I will need to talk to the General and formulate a plan. What would you need from us to make this happen and how long would it take?" she demanded

"Well, that depends on several things. How far away is Sea Town? What is the terrain like on the way? How many people are we taking? How far away were the troops and when will they arrive at Sea Town?"

Nirvana nodded, "Rosa, ensure Will has everything he needs to get the General, his team and all of the Medicas we can spare to Sea Town. It is 50 len from here and the ground rises at first, to get over the Demon's Head Hills, but then it falls as it gets closer to the sea." Nirvana reported. "As for the number of people, General, could you give an idea of the amount of people needed?"

Will recognised the General as the one who had been going to execute him on his first meeting with the Council. He was tall and powerful, but somehow graceful. When he had pulled Will's head back, Will had felt a heat coming from his hand. At the time he hadn't really thought much about it as he was a little busy being executed. But, afterwards, Rosa had told him that General Ember was a salamander. Whilst he was humanoid in form, he was able to withstand great heat, and could also generate fire when needed.

The discussions went on for some time and, once Will had converted len into miles, he came up with a list of supplies he would need to get one of his engines running. The General had told Will that they would need to use his biggest engine, the Garratt, but when Will told the council how much coal he would need to run the massive machine they had baulked.

"That would wipe out our whole store. We can mine more but it takes time and that is something we don't have at the moment" Nirvana had responded.

So, Will had decided upon Number 4 as this engine was built to pull heavy trains over the Austrian Alps and so was used to gradients like those of the Demon's Head Range.

A few of the council members were not happy with the use of a "human machine". Veneema was particularly vocal about it but, in the end, they realised that Will and Number 4 were their only hope of rescuing the people of Sea Town. By the time the discussion was complete, it was late evening. It would take the rest of the night and most of the following day to prepare the engine and the supplies needed. So, it was agreed that they would set off as darkness fell the next night. That would also give the added bonus of keeping the Allied Magiks' movements secret for a little while longer.

That night, no-one slept. There was so much to prepare and so little time. Coal had to be brought from where it was stored at the mines. Troops and medicas had to be briefed and given equipment and most importantly of all, Number 4 had to be made ready. Carts were gathered and reinforced for the journey. They weren't made to be towed behind an engine and would be moving faster than usual. The speed made the journey rougher and so, made the carts more vulnerable to damage. Carpenters worked throughout the day and night in order to make the carts fit for purpose. In the end, they had 50 carts and close to 300 troops and medicas on board.

At first light they would set off. Will couldn't help but feel elated to be in the cab of a steaming train again. He knew that the situation was dire, but feeling the power of the engine, watching the steam rise from the chimney, it just felt right. However, he was also nervous. He was only an apprentice engineman. He had never driven an engine alone, on a long distance journey before. He had been the fireman for a while and had been alongside other drivers many times but driving on his own was a big task. He had always had experienced enginemen with him in the past and the crew who were with him today were complete novices. So'Ren was acting as his fireman. Will wasn't so worried about him as the young lizard man seemed to intuitively understand the engine and its workings. But his other crew member was Rosa. Will wasn't entirely sure of her role in driving the engine, but it seemed that wherever So'Ren went, Rosa was too. Or maybe it was the other way around. Anyhow, she was in the cab with them and wasn't too bad at taking instructions. General Ember rode in the cab too, but Will was fairly sure that he wasn't going to be taking any orders, only giving them. So'Ren and Rosa knew that Will was worried about the journey and they did their best to encourage him and, slowly but surely, the tasks needed to get Number 4 ready were ticked off the list.

The folk of the City of Hope were amazed at the massive, hissing beast that was Number 4. At first there was fear at the noise and heat the engine produced. But, gradually, that fear turned into excitement and the hope that they could actually save Sea Town and its residents. They were also changing their minds about the young driver of this magnificent machine. The story of Will's offer of help in the liberation of Sea Town had spread like wildfire, throughout the City of Hope. Folk struggled to believe that a human was going to help them. But help them he did and the frowns of disbelief began to change into smiles and grins when folk realised that they were going to take the fight to King Starin. And this time, they had a chance at winning!

As the sun started to set, the final wagon was attached to the engine and the safety valves lifted. The train gradually pulled out of the hastily constructed siding and steamed off into the rapidly darkening countryside of Vitae. Their first stop would be to collect water, but that wasn't going to be for a while, so Will settled into the task of running Number 4 as efficiently as he could. He was pleased to find that, once he got over his nerves, he had no problem with driving the engine. He had seen it done so many times and had been the engine's driver too. OK, so he had been supervised every other time, but he had to go solo at some point so it might as well be tonight. When they had first set off, Will had steadied his nerves by telling So'Ren all about the history of Number 4. How it had been built in 1889, in a country called Austria during a time of world wars and how, after almost 90 years service, it was sold to another, then another country, until it was so out of date that it couldn't be used on the mainline any more. That was when the Ginger Line had bought it and restored it to the amazing machine it was today. The young lizard man was really interested in the story and encouraged Will to keep talking.

Rosa was not so interested and had gone to sit on the roof of the engine to be another pair of lookout eyes. She might not have been interested in Will's story, but she did enjoy listening to Will's voice and these feelings confused her. Will was still a human after all and humans and her folk didn't get on. Did they?

Nirvana had asked her friend Crroona to travel with the rescue party. Crroona was an owl griffin, with the body of a wolf and the head of an owl. Her night vision was unrivalled so, having her sat on the buffer of Number 4, looking out for damaged tracks and attacks from Starin's army, gave the whole party a sense of safety. If they were attacked, the extra minutes notice that Crroona could give them might make the difference between victory and defeat.

5
INTO THE FIRE

Despite their best efforts, by the time the train arrived at Sea Town, Starin's army had arrived and started destroying the buildings and herding up its residents like sheep. There were magik-users in Sea Town; mermaids and lizard folk were a common sight in the seaside town. Their numbers were low, and they were only able to protect small areas, where the most vulnerable had been told to gather. The hospital and town council building still held strong, but many of the other buildings were reduced to rubble by the weapons of Starin's army.

Nirvana had managed to get word to the town that a metal dragon was on its way to evacuate folk and that they should ensure that the cart tracks were in good shape. The town's council had been confused by this, but they did what they could. Nirvana was well-respected in these parts and her message had given them hope. Until that point, folk had thought fighting was useless as they couldn't hope to win against Starin's trained soldiers. But, they had fought back as hard as they could, to give Nirvana's dragon the time it needed to get to them. Starin's soldiers were surprised by the resistance of Sea Town's folk. They weren't used to actually having to fight hard against an enemy. These soldiers fought because they had to. Because, if they didn't, they feared what would happen to their friends and families. This all meant that the attack on Sea Town had been less than successful by the time the folk of the Allied Magiks arrived. The sight of the steaming engine took them completely by surprise and, when the troops of the Allied Magiks leapt from the train's wagons, their advance fell apart.

In no time at all, the Allied Magiks combined their powers and constructed a magikal wall of energy to protect the fleeing residents from the arrows and missiles fired from the weapons of the human soldiers. The energy wall was a new tactic that had been developed by General Ember and this was the first time he had the opportunity to put it to use. It was a huge success and saved many lives that day. General Ember deployed his troops, all of whom were magik-wielders, and they quickly dispersed the already demoralised army. Some surrendered to the Allied Magiks, but most fled to a place of safety, to await instructions from their general.

Once the worst of the assault had passed, the folk of Sea Town started to pour out of the ruined town, towards Number 4 and their rescuers. On first seeing Will, a ripple of terror ran through them. Some turned to run back into the town, but Rosa swiftly addressed them.

"Will is the one who organised this rescue. Do not judge him by the actions of Starin's humans. Will is not from Vitae and he does not hold with their actions. He is one of us and has been accepted by Nirvana and the council of the City of Hope."

This announcement stunned the folk of Sea Town. A

human as a member of the folk of Vitae! It was unheard of. But, such was the respect they had for Nirvana, that they lost some of their fear and started to inspect the engine instead.

General Ember was keen to load the train and get out of the area as quickly as they could. He knew that Starin's troops hadn't fully left the area and he knew they had to evacuate. He was unsure what he should do with the human troops who had surrendered and so approached Rosa to discuss a plan of action.

"We don't have the space to take them with us," Rosa advised.

"I know. But we can't just leave them here. I don't think we have any choice but to execute them," Ember replied.

"What?! You can't do that. They are living, breathing beings who surrendered to you!" Will spluttered in disbelief.

"We don't have the resources to guard them, we can't take them with us and if we release them, they will return to their army and be executed by their own people. So how is it any different if we execute them? This is war, Will. There are no good choices" Ember told him.

"Look at them. Do they look like hardened fighting men who signed up for this war to you? To me, they look like frightened boys who have had no choice but to join the fighting. Just talk to them. They may surprise you."

"We don't have time for this. Starin's army are just over that ridge and could attack at any moment," Ember retorted.

But Rosa stood staring at the humans for a moment and then nodded at Will.

"You are right, Will. We need to be better than Starin. If we want this war to ever end, we need to show the humans that we are not the enemy that Starin claims we are. Come,

Ember. Let us see what they have to say."

The general deployed his troops to guard the evacuation and defence of the folk of Sea Town and then, reluctantly, followed Rosa and Will to where the human prisoners were being held. Rosa was the first to speak.

"I am Rosa of the City of Hope. Which of you speaks for the others?"

The humans looked confused for a moment, and then one stepped forward and addressed Rosa, Will and Ember. He looked to be little more than a teenager and completely out of his league!

"Errr well I suppose that would be me. I am Owen Trelisker. Second Sword, Company of the Fist. "

"How old are you, Owen Trelisker?" Ember asked.

"I have seen 15 summers, Sir" he replied. "I was made second sword for this battle."

Will, Rosa and Ember were shocked at the age of the boy. He was far too young to be fighting in a battle. They looked at the other prisoners and many were of a similar age. Some were even younger!

"Why do you fight? You should still be in school," Rosa asked.

"If we don't join the army, our families don't eat. When we join up, a bounty of 100 credits is given to our families. That can feed them for a year. They get another 100 credits every first day. I do not know what will happen to my Mother now. There is only the two of us..." Owen trailed off, as if suddenly realising the extent of what he had done.

Rosa and Will glanced at each other. They both felt terrible for Owen and for his mother. But what could they do? Then, Will had an idea.

He led Ember and Rosa a short distance away and outlined his hastily thought up plan.

“Let him kill one of us.”

“WHAT??????”

“Not actually kill one of us, I mean make it look like they surrendered in order to get close enough to kill one of us. Then they can rejoin their army as heroes. You said it yourself, we can’t take them with us and if we do this, we give them a chance of not being executed by their own people. Not only that but having soldiers in the army who could discreetly plant the seed that we aren’t the bad guys, might be useful in the future.”

“Actually Will, that isn’t bad. We can’t release them all. It would look too suspicious. But, if we kept some prisoners and released the rest we could march them back to our City. Make use of them. Manual labour and all that. What do you think, Rosa?”

“It’s risky. But, I think it could work and, if the troops on the ridge over there see us treating the prisoners that we take with us with respect, maybe they will start to see us in a better light. It may only make a few less hostile, but it’s a start. Let’s do it. How are they going to kill me? Don’t start, General. I am the highest profile of the folk here so it has to be me. We don’t have time to discuss this. Let’s just get it done.”

The general nodded and they quickly put together the plan. Once they all knew what they were doing, the general and Rosa headed off towards the prisoners and Will headed back to the engine. The prisoners were herded towards Number 4 and Rosa ensured that Owen was close enough that he could hear Will’s whispered voice. At first Owen couldn't understand what Will was asking him, but after a couple of tries, he got it. His face paled visibly but then he spoke to a few of the soldiers around him. They started shuffling about and resisting having their hands bound. Then all of a sudden, a fight broke out and Starin's young soldiers were doing more of the hitting than the Vitaens were!

Suddenly, Owen bellowed and charged into Will, knocking him down and, in turn knocking the wind out of him.

"Steady mate. You don't have to kill me too," Will whispered.

Owen grabbed the knife that Will had tucked in his belt and leapt to his feet. Then he ran. Will blinked once and the boy was gone! Then he realised that he might have made a huge mistake. What if Owen wasn't just an unfortunate boy who was worried about his mother? What if he really killed Rosa? What if...

Shut up Will lad and get off your butt. Will leapt up and started running towards Rosa and Ember. He was just about to shout a warning, when he saw Owen. He was right behind Rosa. Before Will could even think, Owen had drawn the knife over Rosa's throat and she had dropped to the ground. Lifeless.

"ROSAAAAAAA, " Will screamed.

For a moment, everything in Will's field of vision stopped. It was like all of the lights around him had gone out, but there was a locomotive headlamp on and it was shining directly at Rosa, lying there on the ground. It was the only thing he could see.

Then, very slowly and precisely, Rosa winked at him. Will's knees buckled and the next thing he knew he was sitting on the floor. He suddenly became aware of everything that was going on around him. General Ember was rallying the troops against an oncoming Army that was charging down from the hills surrounding the town. He was bellowing at Will to get Number 4 moving, NOW, whilst carrying Rosa's 'lifeless' body up and throwing her, unceremoniously into the cab of the engine.

Will leapt to his feet and into the cab after Rosa. The engine was ready to move, it just needed to be put into motion. So'Ren was already shovelling coal into the fire, looking angry and relieved at the same time. He hadn't known about the hastily arranged plan to trick the enemy general and had just watched his best friend get killed. As he shovelled coal, Rosa was lying in a snotty heap on the floor frantically whispering to her friend that she was sorry and that everything would be alright.

"Rosa, aren't you going to get up?" Will asked.

"Not yet, they might be watching. I have to stay dead for a while longer yet," she whispered back. "By the way, that was amazing acting out there. If I hadn't known it was all part of the plan, I would have thought I was dead!"

Will blushed bright red and mumbled something about the school panto, then he set to work getting the engine safely away. Suddenly, out of the corner of his eye, he saw one of Starin's troops charging towards Number 4. He had his sword raised and was hell bent on trying to kill the engine's occupants. Will frantically looked around for a weapon, a knife, a gun anything. Then So'Ren handed him his shovel. Will looked at it, looked at So'Ren then looked at the oncoming soldier. The penny dropped and he swung the shovel as hard as he could, striking the soldier on his steel helmet.

CLANG!!! The vibrations shot up Will's arms and he almost fell out of the cab in shock.

So'Ren was hopping up and down congratulating Will on a job well done and grabbing his shovel back so he could continue working the fire, urged on by Will shouting

"I didn't tell you to stop shovelling."

Will turned back to the controls and blew the whistle to let the Allied Magiks know it was time to go. The folk made a last effort to disengage from the enemy army and leapt back into the carts, firing magical shots the whole time. Will threw open the regulator and, with a lot of wheel spin, they were off. For a while the enemy army tried to keep up, but as the engine picked up speed, they quickly fell behind.

A small contingent of Allied Magiks' troops had left during the melee with the prisoners of war. They were being marched back to the City of Hope and would be put to work until it had been decided what to do with them. Will prayed that they hadn't been noticed leaving as they would make an excellent target for Starin's troops.

Will and So'Ren didn't talk much during the journey back to the City of Hope. They were pushing themselves, and the engine, to the max, trying to get as far away from Starin's troops as possible and get the refugees to the safety of the city. After many hours of travelling, stopping to fill up the water tanks and pick up coal from the dumps that the dwarves had put in place for them, they arrived back at the magical barrier which protected the city. General Ember quickly opened the portal and they rushed inside.

The relief that Will felt when that portal closed was immense. It washed over him like a warm shower and he gave a huge sigh of relief. So'Ren dropped down to the floor and sat gasping for breath. Even with Will helping with shovelling the coal when he could, the effort of keeping the engine moving at top speed had been exhausting for the young lizard man. Rosa had been helpfully telling him to put his back into it and stop being so lazy. She had remained in her snotty heap on the floor, just in case anyone had been watching. In order to keep up the illusion that Rosa had been killed at Sea Town, Will picked her up and threw her over his shoulder. Ember had gone on ahead to fill Nirvana in on their deception. Given how unhelpful she had been throughout the journey home, Will made sure to be none too gentle with Rosa.

"Oops! Sorry! Who put that wall there? Sorry, was that your head that hit the handle. Wow! That must have hurt. Sorry!"

"When you put me down, you had better run. Fast!" Rosa whispered in reply. Will and So'Ren had to work very hard to keep their faces straight! They carried Rosa to the council chambers, where they were met by a very sombre looking Nirvana. She stood back from the door and let them pass in before her. Then, once the door was shut, Rosa leapt from Will's shoulder and gave him a kick on the backside.

"Told you to run!" She laughed but then saw Nirvana's disapproving frown. "Sorry, Mother."

General Ember had ensured that the majority of the council members were not in the cabin when Will, Rosa and So'Ren had entered. As Master of Spies for the Allied Magiks, Stormwind was present.

"Stormwind, I have a gift and a task for you," the general began. "The gift is a young human boy called Owen

Trelisker. The task is to find a way to contact him. He is a Second Sword in the Company of the Fist and he is going to help us win this war."

Stormwind was silent for a moment as he took in the enormity of what Ember had just told him. His mind was whirring with possibilities.

"Well, Ember. That is a kind and generous gift and I am very grateful for your bounty. I do have some ideas of how to contact this Owen and will happily take on the task. I have a ...friend, shall we say, who works in the barracks and may be able to help us out."

As Stormwind spoke, his excitement grew. Having a spy in Starin's army would be huge.

"Do you realise what this means? We finally have a way in. A way to learn some of Starin's plans, but also a way to quietly dispel some of Starin's propaganda about us. One person, in the right position, could win this war for us. Owen's knowledge and position within Starin's Army may well be invaluable if we are going to finally defeat Starin. We are going to defeat Starin, aren't we?" Stormwind finally stopped speaking and looked around at the others in the room.

Nirvana gave Stormwind a smile and nodded. With Owen Trelisker working with them and the additional support of Will and his engines, Nirvana knew that there had never been a better time to take the fight to the humans.

6

TECHNOLOGY FROM AFAR

King Starin sat at the desk in his office, glowering at the report he had just received from General Watkins. Watkins had overseen the attack on Sea Town. The failed attack on Sea Town. Not only had Watkins failed to exterminate the magik-users in the town, but a human had been assisting the magik scum. A human with a steam locomotive! Starin could not understand where this human had come from or how the magik-users had managed to get their hands on a piece of technology that advanced. If they had one locomotive, did they have more? How had they figured out how to use them and who was that human?

Starin threw his chair back and stormed out of the office. His guards leapt out of his way. They knew only too well that Starin could take drastic action when he was this angry. Despite this, they also knew that they had to follow behind him, wherever he went and he was going to the warehouse. A huge building, hidden away in the bowels of the castle that few knew about. Only Starin, his bodyguards and his closest advisors had ever been in the warehouse. It contained a massive collection of strange and otherworldly objects and only these advisors knew where they had come from.

Starin approached a small, shabby room, in which sat a dirty, hairy man in stained overalls who looked as if he hadn't washed in a year. This was Havesh, the chief engineer.

"Give me a progress report," Starin demanded.

"Yes Sir. Operation Downfall is moving forward as expected. We should be ready to go in 30, hmm maybe 40 days," Havesh replied. He spoke in a distracted way and didn't seem to be intimidated by Starin's presence. The guards weren't sure if they were more scared of Starin or Havesh. Starin was cruel and hateful but Havesh, Havesh was on another level. He was a genius and could make anything he set his mind to.

What the guards didn't know was that Havesh was a half breed; part human and part magik user. Starin had captured him and his family many years ago and tortured him until he had agreed to do as Starin ordered. Havesh had been under no illusions that Starin would also torture his family if he didn't do exactly as the king commanded and, over the years, it had slowly driven him mad. His family must have been long gone but, as the magik side of his genetics gave him a greater lifespan than humans, he lived on. Now he did as Starin commanded out of misguided anger towards his magik. The magik that had kept him alive for so long without his beloved Mira, a human, and the beautiful children she had given him; anger that his people had not come to rescue him. Anger at losing his home and friends and family. Havesh was not only angry though, he was also curious. He was an engineer and the devices and technology that Starin found on occasion fascinated him. They were obviously not from this world. The materials and level of technology were well beyond anything Vitae had to offer. Where they came from Havesh did not know, but when Starin told him to start taking them apart to see how they worked, he had eagerly complied.

On hearing how long Operation Downfall was going to take, Starin became even angrier than he had been when he entered the warehouse.

"40 days! I don't have 40 days. The scum have found a locomotive and used it against my troops. If they have found more than one we will lose any advantage that we currently have."

"They have a locomotive? Where from? How do they know how to use it?"

"They had a human with them. I can only assume that he brought the engine and that he knows how it works." Starin replied. "He cannot be from Vitae."

"Not from Vitae? Where else could he be from?" Havesh asked. When Starin was this angry, it was sometimes possible to get him to give away little titbits of information. Information is power and Havesh needed power.

"There are many worlds out there. Did you think we were alone in the universe? I thought you were more intelligent than that!" Starin sneered. "I want Downfall ready in no more than 20 days. If it is not, you will no longer be of use to me." Starin strode out of the warehouse in a fury and without realising, knocked aside a tapestry that hung on the wall. Havesh waited for the King's party to leave and then went to look at the place where the tapestry had previously been hanging. In an alcove in the wall stood a metal shield, bearing a crest.

"Hmmmm, what does that say. I can't quite... where is that lamp?" Havesh found an oil lamp and brought it over to the alcove and continued muttering to himself. "Now then. Great Highland Narrow Gauge Railway. Hmmm, I wonder what that means."

Starin's son, Prince Steele, had the misfortune to be in his father's line of sight at the moment he left the warehouse. Steele was a constant disappointment to his father. Not strong enough, not intelligent enough and certainly not ruthless enough. However, Steele was well-regarded by his men, who thought him an excellent officer, which drove them to become a very successful company within Starin's Army.

"Good morning, Father," Steele greeted him, coming smartly to attention and saluting.

"Get out of my way." Starin screamed, barging past his son without a backwards glance.

"Okay then," Steele remarked quietly. "Not such a good morning!"

Steele was used to Starin's outbursts and they rarely bothered him anymore. He had no respect for the king at all as his cruelty was legendary.

Steele's mother had been a calm and loving woman, but had been thrown out of the castle on Steele's seventh naming day and told never to return.

"Your mother has done her duty and is no longer necessary. All women know how to do is produce offspring and she has done that. From now on you will behave like a man and learn to kill those who oppose my rule,"Starin had told him.

Steele had studied hard and once he finished his education, had joined the army as a junior officer.

Steele continued to walk away from his father and headed over to where his men were billeted. Every morning he conducted an inspection of their barracks and kit.

"How are you this morning First Sword Wells?"

"Good, sir. Thank you. There is a blockage in the pipes in the barracks though. The smell is pretty strong, sir," Wells grimaced.

"OK. Contact the Quartermaster and have it repaired. If he hasn't been down by close of business today, let me know and I will kick his butt. In the meantime, use the facilities in Company of the Bear Barracks. They are away on patrol at the moment. Tell the men to leave it tidy. I don't want any complaints."

"Thank you, sir. I am sure the men will be pleased."

Back in the City of Hope, Will was cleaning Number 4 after its long journey. He had plenty of oil in the cans that were always stored on each engine, but he knew this wouldn't last forever. He would have to talk to So'Ren about finding something similar for when his stock ran out. Will knew that the engines would all be in use from now on.

Once the rescue party had arrived back in the City of Hope, Nirvana had demanded a debrief and once she had heard how much of a difference Will and his engines had made, she had insisted that at least one engine be ready to go at all times. Given the amount of coal that the Garratt needed, this meant that the bulk of the work would fall on Number 4 and the Darjeeling, working one week at a time each.

Will had to admit that he was worried. Having to keep the two engines in a constant state of readiness was a lot of work. He knew that he would need help and, whilst So'Ren was a great engineer, even he wasn't going to be up to the challenge of keeping things running. Will knew that he needed to train up more Folk. He would have to speak to Nirvana about it but knew it wasn't an easy task. Most were training for the army; preparing themselves for the battle to come. Rosa had offered to help with the maintenance, but it was fairly obvious that she wasn't mechanically-minded. Her talents lay in other areas, like hitting things really hard and leading companies in the Army of Vitae.

During one of Rosa's helping sessions, she mentioned that she had seen Will's attempts to defend his engine with the shovel and that she thought he had been incredibly brave. Will blushed a beautiful red colour and muttered something about "doing the right thing."

In order to stop Rosa embarrassing him anymore Will blurted out

"Well, you looked beautiful when you were fighting. You are so graceful." Now, Will wasn't the only one blushing. Rosa joined him on the beetroot scale.

"Sorry, that was a bit out of line. Sorry Rosa."

"Don't apologise. I think that is the nicest thing anyone has ever said to me!" After a bit of embarrassed silence and neither of them knowing where to look, Rosa had started to ask Will about the engines.

"You really love these engines, don't you?"

"I do. They are the closest thing I have to a family, I guess. To me, they feel alive. Each one has a personality all of its own. They tell me when they feel good, when something isn't right, when they need feeding or a drink."

Rosa didn't really understand any of what Will was

saying, but she respected him enough to know that what he was telling her was his truth. She just loved to hear him talking.

"Well, I should let you get on. I know how busy you are, and I don't want to stop you working. But, if you would like, I can teach you to fight and defend yourself. We may even be able to find you a better weapon than a shovel. Only if you want to though," she told him.

Without waiting for a reply, Rosa slipped out of the engine shed and crept back to her cabin, careful to ensure she wasn't seen, in order to maintain the illusion of her death. As she went, her mind was buzzing. She couldn't understand what it was about Will that made her feel all warm and fuzzy inside.

7

I Didn't Know They Were Real!

Following on from the request from the Council, Will and his engines were worked really hard over the next few weeks. Each time he was given a task he, and his engines, proved invaluable to the Folk of the City of Hope. But every time Will left the security of the city, he was conscious of how vulnerable he was and was embarrassed that Nirvana had to send a bodyguard with him as he was unable to protect himself. So, after he had finished his day's work, Will went to find Rosa. She was in the clearing outside of her home, going through the intricate, and exhausting yoga style training that the kitsune used to hone their fighting skills. Will had improved dramatically in this skill over the past few weeks, but Rosa still had to put in extra time to ensure that she was getting the workout that her muscles needed. Added to that, Rosa needed to keep a low profile if she was going to protect Owen Trelisker. There was always the possibility that Starin had spies within the City of Hope and it was vital that news of Rosa's miraculous recovery from the usually permanent condition of death didn't reach King Starin. Keeping out of sight was boring and all Rosa felt she could do was train harder and read as many books on tactics as she could lay her hands on.

She also spent a lot of time talking to Will about Vitae and how it differed from his world. Will had been fascinated by Rosa's use of her elemental magik during their last battle and had asked her to tell him more about it.

"We can use it in so many ways. Some of the folk are born with the ability to use one of the elements; fire, earth, air and water. Some are born with more than one ability. Once in a while, someone is born with the ability to use all the elements. I am one of those folk. I can charge my weapons with fire which allows me to cut through hard substances, like armour. I can use air and water in the same way, or to knock someone off balance and I can, make the ground move with earth. Obviously, they aren't just for use in battle, they can be used at other times. However, I do use them most in battle. Let us hope that will change soon," Rosa explained.

When Rosa saw Will approaching, she couldn't help but smile. He was always able to cheer her up. Right now though, he looked a little worried.

"What's wrong Will?" she asked.

"Nothing really. I just wondered if.....well if you were still willing to teach me how to fight. I feel so useless when I go out on missions. I have to take up the time of some of the folk which could be put to much better use. I am sure they would rather be doing anything other than babysitting me?"

"Babysitting? What is this? You mean acting as your

bodyguard? That is a privilege for them! You are very important to this fight, as are your engines. It is vital that you are kept in one piece."

Will didn't really believe Rosa, but he smiled and nodded and they set about training.

Rosa and Will trained together, every day from that day forward. At first, Will was frustrated that he wasn't learning to fight, but Rosa quickly explained that learning to defend yourself rarely involves just punching and kicking.

"You need to be able to take the punches and kicks too. Protecting yourself is as important as taking out your opponent."

It didn't take long for Will to realise just how much stronger the kitsune are than humans. Rosa's strength amazed him, but it wasn't just her. One day, during one of their regular training sessions, a kitsune named Liam approached Rosa and told her that Nirvana had asked to see her. Liam offered to continue working with Will until Rosa got back. Now, it has to be said that Liam was not the largest of the kitsune. In fact, Will thought he looked like a child.

However, when he started to teach Will, it became very obvious who was the stronger of the pair. Kitsune were also incredibly nimble and could use their speed to evade their opponents. They used their tails to improve their balance and agility, but they could also be used as a weapon. When angry, or during a fight, kitsune wound their nine tails together so tightly that it appeared as just one tail. This single tail was then used to great effect, as a club or to trip someone up. Will had found this out during one of the training sessions with Rosa. He had also discovered that her tail was wonderfully soft and fluffy, but that was another matter!

Nirvana occasionally watched Rosa and Will training. She never let them know that she was there, just watched from a distance. Over time, she could see their relationship developing. She was worried for her daughter as she knew that Will would have to return to his world one day and Rosa would have her heart broken. Nirvana also worried that Will was a human. After generations of hating humans, it was so hard to just put those feelings aside. She had to stop her mind from going to the familiar place of hatred and to accept that Will was as good as he seemed. Rosa was no fool, even if she hadn't realised that she was falling in love with Will. If Rosa was happy, Nirvana would do her best to be happy too.

Over the next few days, Will and So'Ren continued to work on the Darjeeling.

"Why is she called Sherpa, Will?"

"Sherpa's are a race of people who come from a place called Nepal, which is a neighbour of Darjeeling. They are an amazing race of people who are known throughout my world for their climbing ability. They can carry loads to the highest places and are so strong. So, this engine is just like them. Strong and a great climber. It just seemed fitting to call her Sherpa."

A coach had been fitted to Sherpa so that folk from the City of Hope could take a ride behind the engine and see what all the fuss was about. Will drove the engine backwards and forwards through the city, several times a day to ensure it was always ready to go into action, should the need arise. Will knew that Rosa watched the engine from her place of hiding and it always made him smile to think of her starting to love the locomotives. For some reason, it mattered to him that Rosa liked the things he liked.

On one such occasion, Nirvana appeared at Rosa's shoulder and chuckled at her daughter looking longingly at the engine.

"Are you watching your future mate again, Rosa?"

"My what?" Rosa spluttered in reply. "Will and I are friends. I am teaching him to defend himself and he is teaching me to better understand humans. That is all."

Nirvana laughed again. She could see how fond the two youngsters were of each other. Despite her wariness of humans in general, she was happy to finally see her daughter falling for someone. Especially someone like Will. In that moment Nirvana made a decision.

"Rosa, as you know, operations are going to become more frequent and more complex. We are going to need someone to lead the new Railway Defence Force and I am appointing you to the role. You start immediately. Of course, for now, you will have to wear some kind of disguise. We don't want news of your amazing recovery from death to get back to Starin!"

"Me? Mother... I don't know what to say. How many troops will I be commanding?"

"That is yet to be decided. We will have to discuss the Force with Will so we can see what he needs. He certainly needs more drivers and folk to fix these engines. The poor boy looks exhausted. Let us meet in the council chambers in an hour. I will get a message to Will."

Suddenly, the cloaking shield which hid the City of Hope from prying eyes opened and a badly injured, ape-like creature called a sasquatch came hobbling through. He was bellowing and screaming like a banshee, begging for help. Then, his strength gave out and the sasquatch collapsed on the tracks, right in front of Will's train.

In a flash, Will had slammed on the brakes, causing the train to come to a sudden and violent stop, with the horrible sound of screeching metal, and leapt out of the cab to try and help in any way he could. Nirvana, and a cloaked figure, quickly arrived, having forced their way through the crowd that was growing larger every moment that passed. Nirvana had ensured that the shield was back up and had immediately raced to the fallen creature.

Medicas had been summoned and they quickly arrived to assess the sasquatch's injuries. They were nothing short of horrific. Many of his bones were broken, he was covered in lash marks and what looked like burns and not one part of his body wasn't covered in bruises. He was raving and shouting, but no-one there could understand what he was saying. The medicas rushed him off to the infirmary almost as soon as they arrived.

Once the crowd had been moved on, Nirvana indicated that they should all meet in the council chambers as quickly as they could. Will climbed back into the cab of Sherpa and took it back to the shed. So'Ren told him that he would make sure the engine was taken care of so Will could head straight over the meeting with Nirvana.

As he arrived, Nirvana and Rosa, still in her cloak, were discussing what they had just witnessed.

"He has obviously been tortured. I have never seen injuries like that before."

"Nor I, daughter. In all my hundreds of years, I have never seen the like."

"Hundreds of years? You don't look a day over 30," Will quipped as he walked into the chamber. He didn't really feel much like joking but, as he assumed Nirvana was joking about her age, he responded in kind.

"Ahhh Will. How kind. I am not a child of 30 but a woman of 376 summers. We are a race that lives many, many times longer than you humans."

This earned a shocked expression from Will, but before he could ask any further on the subject, Nirvana continued speaking, "Now, we are here to discuss what just happened and to discuss the new Railway Defence Force which Rosa is to command."

"Railway Defence Force? What is that?" Will asked.

"It is a company of troops who are there, purely to defend your engines and the tracks that they travel on. The metal workers and masons are, as we speak, improving the tracks to take the weight of your engines, the dwarves are going to meet your needs in terms of coal. At least for now, anyway. In the long term, we must find a more efficient way of heating the water you need.

I also need to find folk who can learn to drive the engines so that you can have a break from the work. We cannot afford for you to be too exhausted to work."

"I was thinking something similar, and I had an idea. The folk here want to train to fight and you need their numbers if you have any hope of taking the battle to Starin. But, what about the prisoners that we brought from Sea Town? They arrived the other day and, since then, have had nothing to occupy their minds, or their hands. Let's train them to be engineers and drivers. They already have some military training and so would be a great start for the Railway

Defence Force. I know some of them wouldn't be suitable but many of the young ones don't support Starin's regime. They fought because they had no choice." Will blurted all of this out without stopping. He was afraid that Nirvana would think it a ridiculous plan and wanted to get it all out before she stopped him!

For a moment, Nirvana just stared at him. But then, she nodded.

"I was wondering where to get that much manpower, but your plan is a good one. "

"Pardon?"

"Your plan is good. I approve. I will have General Ember decide which of the prisoners are suitable for the Force and the two of you can work together to create the Railway Defence Force.

Now, onto the Sasquatch. Yes Will, that was a sasquatch."

"Funny, I didn't think his feet looked that big!" Rosa and Nirvana gave Will a questioning look and he went on "Sorry, in the United States, a country in my world, they also use the term "Big Foot" when talking about sasquatches. His feet didn't look that big though. Anyway, I am rambling. Sorry. I guess I miss home a little bit!"

Nirvana nodded her understanding of Will's emotions and then moved on. They discussed the obvious torture of the Sasquatch but without more information there was little they could do.

"We must wait until the medicas say we can speak to him before we can learn anymore," Nirvana confirmed.

It was not until the next afternoon that the medicas told Nirvana that she could come and see the sasquatch. Will and, (a suitably disguised), Rosa went along with Nirvana to learn what they could about how he found his way to the City of Hope. Stormwind, the master of spies, met them at the infirmary and they went in together. The sasquatch was in a lot of pain still and looked like death warmed up, but he was keen to tell his story.

His name was Boorlaag and he lived in the high passes of the Dragon's Teeth Mountains, far to the north of the City of Hope. One day, a company of soldiers had come to his home and captured many of his people. They wanted to use the strength of the sasquatch in their mines. But sasquatches cannot stand to be under the ground. They need to be in the open, under the sky. Most of his people fell sick and died. The remaining few were sent to a camp and were forced to work night and day. They were given never-ending hard labour and little food or rest. They were beaten and tortured every day. One day Boorlaag had fallen asleep when he should have been unloading a cart of supplies. He was beaten almost to death. In fact, the guards must have thought him dead because they left him where he fell, like rubbish. Boorlaag had escaped and made his way to the City of Hope, which he had been told of by some of the other prisoners. They had told him of the shield and how to get through it. This made Stormwind sit up. He recognised the flaw in their security immediately. Boorlaag went on for many hours, telling of the torture and mistreatment of the folk of Vitae at the hands of Starin's people. He told of the disgusting conditions they were made to live in and the unspeakable ways that Starin ensured that he always had enough slaves.

Will felt physically sick at Boorlaag's words. It immediately brought up images of the Second World War concentration camps from the history books he had read back on Earth.

Upon leaving the infirmary, Nirvana gathered the council and immediately started planning a rescue mission. They had to get the Folk of Vitae out of that place. The first thing she did was to call on the aid of an old friend. She went to the highest point in the city; a tower made of stone, where every other building was made of wood. From the top of this tower, Nirvana turned her face to the sky and shouted to the skies.

"Obsidion, friend of Vitae, I call upon you now, to render us aid in a time of great need."

Everyone waited. And waited. And waited. The sun had almost set, and Will was ready to go and get something to eat, when Rosa nudged him in the side.

"Look. Look up you fool. There, see him?"

"What, I can't see anything. Wait, yes I can. Oh my ….. is that a …."

In the distance, getting rapidly closer, was a black, ominous looking shape. At first, Will had thought it was some kind of bird of prey, but it just kept getting bigger and bigger, blacker and blacker.

"A dragon? Yes, it is. Hold on to your hat, this could get intense!"

Finally, the immense creature landed on the field next to the tower and Will got a really good look at his first dragon. Obsidian was well named. His scales looked like pools of black engine oil, gleaming and shining in the sun. The dragon stood at least 20 ft off the ground and had teeth as long as swords. His tail streamed out behind him, making him seem to go on forever. Will had expected the massive to have a booming voice, but when Obsidian did speak, it was with his mind and not his mouth.

"Beloved Nirvana, why have you summoned me? You know I don't like to leave my lair unless it's absolutely necessary," he crooned. His voice was smooth as silk and left Will feeling like honey was running through his mind.

"Ah my darling Obsidian, my people are being harmed and I need your help to stop it. They are being beaten and tortured, by Starin's men in a camp on the plains of Aramanth. We need more information about the camps so that we can bring our might to bear on these infidels and demons. Will you fly high overhead and observe this camp and bring me what I need?"

At the news of the atrocities being performed at the camp, Obsidian grew enraged. He roared his anger into the darkening sky and stomped his feet on the ground.

"Beloved Nirvana. It hurts my heart to hear these fowl tidings. I will not allow the children of your dwellings to be harmed in this way. My kin and I will destroy these evil places and those that there dwell."

"No darling Obsidian. This you must not do! My people remain in the camps and we would rescue them and bring them back to our dwellings for healing."

Will stood, open mouthed, watching the negotiations between Nirvana and Obsidian. After some time Rosa nudged him,

"Close your mouth, you will catch flies!"

"What? Oh! Right. Sorry. I have never... well obviously. Errmmm." Will found himself almost incapable of forming a coherent sentence. The sheer size of the dragon was enough to make his knees wobble, but to have that dragon speaking in his mind was simply, well, mind blowing!

It took Nirvana and Obsidian some time to come to an agreement. Obsidian loved the folk of the City of Hope as their lives had been intertwined since the beginnings of time. Obsidian and his forebears had been known to visit the city on occasion and every leader of the city was formally introduced to the dragons, in their lands, shortly after taking their place at the head of the council. Nirvana had a particularly strong bond with Obsidian and they had always been fond of each other. Obsidian was enraged that Nirvana's folk were being treated badly. Nirvana had to use a lot of flowery language and compliments, but eventually got him to calm down enough to get him to agree to a reconnaissance mission.

Before dawn the next day, Obsidian left with two of his kin. The wait for their return was agonising. Knowing that folk were being tortured whilst those in the City of Hope were comfortable and well fed was a torture all of its own for Will. His mind kept straying to those history books; to the pictures of the Holocaust and the emaciated, beaten, broken bodies of the prisoners of war. When Rosa came to see him that evening, he told her of his fears. She stayed with him long into the night, talking about his world and his love of the engines on the "Ginger Line." She told him about growing up in Vitae and her love of the land she lived on. Her sadness and anger at Starin's abuse of the folk of Vitae. Eventually, they fell asleep under the stars and were only awakened by the rising sun.

Another day passed whilst waiting to hear back from the dragons. Will spent the day with So'Ren and his engines, ensuring they were ready for the upcoming mission. Some of the prisoners from the Sea Town battle came to see where they were going to be working for the foreseeable future and that took Will's mind off his worries for a while.

The following morning, Obsidian returned. He and his kin had watched the camp without rest for the 2 days. They could only watch from on high, for fear of being seen and their purpose being guessed by the soldiers below.

"We were able to ascertain their routines and we can work with this," he told the council members, who had once again gathered at the dragon tower.

A plan was formulated and Will was told that the dragons were going to bring coal and water directly to the trains, on the move.

"Why didn't we do that for the Sea Town run then?" Will had asked.

Rosa waited until Obsidian had left before answering Will.

"Dragons are the laziest creatures on Vitae," she explained. "They will only help when they think it is absolutely necessary and if it benefits them. The older they get, the lazier they get. Amber and Jade, the two dragons who were with Obsidian, are very young, in dragon time. Obsidian is only joining us because of his love for Mother."

8

THE DARKNESS

Two days later, during the darkest hour of the night, Sherpa pulled to a stop just below the crest of a hill. The engine's lights were out and a fog further hid them from the view of the camp's guards. Many heavily armed, magik wielding troops from the army of the City of Hope poured from the train's coaches. Rosa leapt down from her perch on the top of Sherpa's cab and firmly told Will and So'Ren to stay where they were.

Will watched Rosa and the troops slip away into the darkness with an overwhelming sense of guilt and dread. Before long, they start to hear the sounds of a battle and to see the dark night sky lit up with explosions and bursts of magik. The shouting of those fighting drifted up through the fog for a long time, but then there was silence, and the silence was deafening.

Will's mind was spinning with fear over what had happened, whether Rosa and the troops were all dead, or laying on the floor injured, or being tortured. Suddenly, he heard someone approaching. He glanced at So'Ren, who had picked up the fireman's shovel and was holding it as if it were a club.

"Great! What am I supposed to use this time?" Will grumbled to himself. Before he had the chance to find his own weapon, a familiar figure strode out of the fog.

"Rosa? Are you OK? You look .....awful!" Will whispered.

"I am OK" she responded automatically. But Will could see that she wasn't. Her face showed the horrors that she had seen, and Will knew that he had to go down there and see them for himself. He reached out and clasped her shoulder.

"Come on. Let's go."

She nodded, grateful for the gesture and placed her hand on top of his and squeezed it.

"It's bad, Will. Are you sure you want to go? I will understand if you want to stay out here," Rosa asked quietly.

"I am going. I may be able to help."

Will started Sherpa's engine, lit her main head lamp, and they made their way down the hill with the little engine's bright light to show them the way. They passed through the camp's large, black gates and the stench hit them.

So'Ren gagged at the assault on his nose.

"Gods Above. What is that stench?"

"It's rotting bodies," Rosa answers with a haunted look in her eyes. "There are mounds of bodies, just left to rot. No graves, or even any dignity. Just piled up and left there."

Rosa turned away from them and took a deep breath through the handkerchief that she had tied around her nose and mouth. On the way down the hill, she had handed Will and So'Ren a piece of material to use to try and block out some of the fumes, but they had been too busy driving the engine and hadn't had time to put them in place. They did so now, but it was too late. No-one that was there that day would ever forget the smell of the camp, or the sights that the saw.

The Allied Magik troops had gathered all of the camp soldiers up and made them clear an area at the centre of the camp. The area had been dominated by stocks and rings in the wall, where prisoners were tied and had obviously been beaten and tortured. The prisoners were released and were being treated by the medicas that had been with the rescuers. The remaining prisoners were gradually being gently rounded up into a group and brought into the newly-cleared area. Most were little more than walking skeletons, all showed signs of the abuse they had suffered whilst at the camp. There were many different creatures amongst them, mostly magik-users, but not all. Some had obviously not been there as long as others and were in better shape and so were able to help, ensuring that no-one was forgotten.

Blankets were being handed out, along with drink pouches which contained healing elixirs. Will had told the council about the damaging effects of trying to feed the prisoners straight away. Their stomachs would not be used to food, and it could make them suffer even more.

Gradually, the Allied Magiks got as many prisoners ready to travel back to the City of Hope as they could and set a contingent of troops up in a defensive position, just in case Starin had got wind of the attack and sent more troops. By the best calculations of General Ember's staff, Starin couldn't get troops to the camp before 3 days had passed, but that was based on the limited intelligence they had.

It turned out that Boorlaag had vastly underestimated the number of prisoners being held at the camp and there was nowhere near enough room on the coaches attached to Sherpa. There were only six coaches coupled to the engine, one of which was a brake van. So, with the dragons keeping a sharp eye out, as many prisoners were loaded onto the coaches as possible. The rest were taken to a makeshift infirmary and tended by the medica contingent who had been assigned to remain in the camp until they had been able to evacuate everyone.

The camp guards were put to work, clearing up the filth in the yards and buildings, digging graves and creating a basic sewerage system. All the dirtiest jobs were given to the guards, particularly those who wore marks of rank on their uniform. Nothing could ever make up for the way they had treated their prisoners, but they were made to experience just a small part of the suffering they had inflicted. Of course, the guards were fed and watered frequently and were allowed to rest after working for a set period. So, where the prisoners had endured the hardest labour, this was nothing more than unpleasant work.

Four days passed before Will, Rosa, So'Ren and a contingent of troops, scientists and medicas arrived back at the camp. This time they had brought more coaches, which had been hastily built after Rosa had asked Obsidian to fly ahead and tell her mother that they would be needed. This meant that Will had had to put the Garratt into action. There was no way that Sherpa could pull enough coaches to bring all the prisoners and troops back to the City of Hope. During those four days, no soldiers from Starin's army had been seen. Jade and Amber, the two young dragons who had flown with Obsidian, had remained with the troops at the camp and had posted a watch throughout those 4 days. They hadn't seen so much as a messenger in the region surrounding the plains of Aramanth. This had meant that the Allied Magiks who had remained at the camp had been able to put their time to good use. The camp was cleaner and the buildings around the central square had been repaired. The prisoners who had still in the camp were looking a bit healthier than they had. They were still traumatised, but they were no longer starving, and their physical wounds had started to heal. These were the fittest of the prisoners; those who seemed not to have been at the camp as long. They had been given clean clothes and allowed to bathe in warm water and this in itself seemed to have given them back some of their personalities. Will was amazed to see some of them laughing together, over a warm drink. It gave him hope that they could fully recover from their horrific experiences.

Will, Rosa and some of the scientists wanted to have a good look around the camp. They wanted to see if they could find out why the camp was there. Starin had never gone to such great lengths before and there had to be a reason for it. They started in the building which had housed the guard commander.

The first room was an office, full of filing cabinets. Each cabinet was absolutely full of drawings and documents and the scientists started rifling through them eagerly. Will headed down the corridor to the next room to see what he could find. As he opened the door, he saw a detailed plan on the wall and written in clear letters "Operation Downfall". The plan was for a piece of machinery, and it was very familiar to Will.

"That looks like the boiler of a steam engine," he

mumbled to himself. He was just heading over to take a closer look when he spotted a flintlock rifle, propped up in the corner of the room. It was a beauty and had been well maintained. He had just picked it up to inspect it when shouting started in the corridor. Will raced out to find Rosa bundling the scientists out of the room and back into the daylight.

"What's going on?" Will shouted.

"Incoming troops. I don't know anything else yet," Rosa replied.

They both ran, ushering scientists as they went.

When they arrived at the Garratt, Ember was waiting for them. He rushed Rosa into the cab. She was still wearing her disguise as they still didn't want anyone to know that she was alive. Owen Trelisker, and any intelligence he might be able to provide them with, was depending on Rosa staying dead!

"General, what is happening?" Rosa asked.

"Obsidian has seen an incoming army. We need to leave."

"How long do we have?"

"Just long enough to get these people into the coaches and get out of here." Ember snapped back. "I don't have time for conversation, Rosa. We need to move. I don't have the troops to mount an all out defence of this camp."

"I'm not arguing, General" Rosa retorted. She had already started moving towards the coaches to help with the evacuation.

Some of the scientists had rushed back to try and collect some of the documents they had found. Will ached to join them but he knew he had to get the Garratt ready to go.

After about an hour of frantic activity, the train was ready to leave. They had managed to evacuate everyone, but there wasn't room for all the troops. Many had volunteered to make their way back to the City of Hope on foot and, as soon as the engines started moving, they ran out onto the plains, and disappeared into the long grass. They were heading for the mines on the edge of the plains as the dwarves would ensure they were safe until Will could get back to them.

As they were preparing to set off, Rosa spotted a flintlock rifle in the corner of the cab and asked Will about it.

"I found it in that building. I thought I might be able to defend myself better if I had it."

"It is a fine weapon. You chose well. What name will you give it?"

"Name?"

"Yes. It is traditional to name your weapon." Rosa stood back and drew her katana from its sheath on her back. "This is Firebringer. My mother gave her to me when I finished my training. She is part of me and feels alive in my hand when I hold her."

Will pondered this for a moment and suddenly, he knew the name that he wanted to give the rifle.

"Vengeance," he said. "The rifle is called Vengeance."

Rosa nodded and gave Will a small smile. She approved of the name, and of the sentiment.

"Vengeance," she repeated.

The train steamed away safely and without the incoming army even knowing that they had been there. The dragons had spotted them coming from a great distance and this had given the Allied Magiks plenty of time to get safely away. Once the train was out of sight of the camp, the dragons had laid waste to it. They blasted it with fire and razed it to the ground. No more of the magical folk of Vitae would ever be held here and whilst they had not got to the bottom of why the camp was there, they took comfort in knowing that it was destroyed and couldn't be put back into use.

When the incoming army got to the camp, ready for their month of duty, they found that nothing was left. They had seen the plume of smoke from a distance, but there was no way that they could have anticipated the utter destruction of the dragons' fire, and rage at the treatment of their beloved friends. It had been all Rosa could do to stop the dragons from decimating the incoming army.

"Beloved Obsidian. Have no fear. Starin will pay for this. His abuse and torture of our people will not go unpunished. But now is not the time. When we strike, it will be with all of the might of the Allied Magiks and Starin will rue the day he crossed us."

Obsidian had thrown back his head and roared into the skies. Jade and Amber had joined in and the sound had been deafening. With that roar, they pledged their support to the war that was now inevitable.

9

KICK INTO HIGH GEAR

When the Garratt, and its passengers, arrived back at the City of Hope, the aura of outrage was palpable. It was well known that Starin had wanted to destroy them, but the concentration camp was a whole new level of evil. Seeing those former prisoners being off loaded and taken to the infirmary, seeing their injuries, hearing their tales of torture and abuse was more than most of the folk could take.

They were not alone. Will had been scarred by what he had seen and felt like he would never recover from the horrors of the camp that he had named Hell's Gate. The name had stuck and now, all folk referred to the camp in that way.

Once the Garratt had arrived and unloaded, Will had busied himself readying Sherpa to go back out to the mines. He wanted to keep busy so that his mind stopped going back there. But Will hadn't rested in 8 days and, in the end, exhaustion caught up with him.

Rosa, concerned at not having seen Will for some time, came to the shed to see how he was doing. She found him curled up in a ball, on the floor of the cab of Sherpa. His face was streaked with tears and his knuckles were bloody and bruised. Will had tried to release his rage by hitting a few walls and the effects of that were clear on his body. Rosa sat down beside Will, placed his head in her lap and gently covered them both with a blanket. There she sat, until Will woke the following day. During the night, Will had been plagued by nightmares, but Rosa had held his hand and whispered comforting words and just held him until he was soothed enough to sleep peacefully again. When he awoke, Will was rested and better able to deal with the horrors in his memory. The nightmares would plague him for the rest of his days, but with Rosa there to help him through, he was able to deal with them.

Once they had returned to the City of Hope, having collected the troops from the mines, Rosa told Will that many of the prisoners had asked to join the Railway Defence Force.

"They want to learn to work with your engines. The engines that brought them to freedom. I think there is also some curiosity about the human who drives the engines too."

Will was surprised by what Rosa was saying. Until that moment, no one, other that So'Ren and Rosa, had showed anything other than a passing interest in the engines.

"That's great news. If we can train up drivers and firemen, we can have more than one engine running at a time. Not to mention that So'Ren and I can have a day off! Rosa? Would you like to learn to drive the engines too?" Will finished up shyly.

Rosa thought for a moment and then said that she would love to learn to drive. Nirvana strolled into the shed at that moment, with a knowing smile on her face, but she quickly returned to a sombre expression as she told Rosa and Will about her plans to intensify the conflict with Starin. Nirvana was going to lay her whole plan out for discussion with them, but, seeing how exhausted they still were following the Hell's Gate campaign, she decided to hold back for a while.

"You two look absolutely terrible. Get something to eat and have a good night's sleep. We can discuss my plans another time."

"Thank you, Mother. I thought I looked pretty good in this outfit!" Rosa replied cheekily.

"Me too!" Will replied and then blushed the brightest shade of red imaginable.

Then, Rosa blushed too.

King Starin was a very unhappy man. Having received the report about the liberation of the concentration camp and having put the messenger to death for daring to bring him such news, he was looking for someone to hurt. He found himself heading for the workshops which were the home of Operation Downfall. Havesh was there, as usual.

"Progress report. NOW!!" Starin screamed.

"I think we are ready," Havesh replied.

What do you mean, "you think we are ready"?"

"We just need to perform the final tests. Are you staying for them?"

"Of course I am. Get on with it then!"

Havesh limped over to the door in the corner of the workshop. He went through and returned dragging a creature which resembled a rabbit person. Her race was called the pooka, a timid but inquisitive race who were sweet natured and loving, though when defending their mates or babies, they were fierce. This was of little interest to Starin and

Havesh though. All they cared about was that she had magik and was, therefore, suitable to be experimented on.

The pooka girl was tied to the wall using chains that had obviously been used for this purpose in the past. Havesh put on a pair of thick leather gloves and then picked up a sword that had been sitting on his worktable. It wasn't a good-looking weapon. Just a shaped piece of metal with a crude wooden handle, but that was all that was needed for this experiment. If it worked, well, the weapons they would create would be legendary.

Havesh pointed the weapon at the pooka and slowly moved towards her.

"The metal interacts with the field that all magik-users have around them. This field vibrates at a certain frequency and when the metal touches the field. Well, you can see for yourself."

Havesh placed the sword just in front of the girl's face and she started to scream in agony. Havesh held it there for long moments, enjoying the screams, and only removed it when the girl collapsed. The moment the sword was taken away, her screams stopped, and she hung there sobbing from the pain.

"Very good," the king drawled. "I like that very much. How many swords can you produce?"

"Thousands! "Havesh replied. "I am limited only by the amount of Steel you have available."

Havesh had developed a spell that, when combined with regular steel, changed a weapon into an implement of torture to any magik-user it came into close contact with. As a minor magik-user himself, this had not been a pain free experiment! He didn't care though. The pain was nothing compared to the pain it would give his folk. Those that abandoned him to a life of slavery at the hands of this lunatic. Havesh had no love for Starin, but he knew that this was the best place for him to get revenge on the folk who forgot him.

"That is not all though." Havesh continued. He pointed to a row of metal tanks lined up on the wall. They were all marked as containing toxic material and connected by pink rubber hoses. Havesh handed Starin a gas mask, which earned the mad scientist a confused look from the king, then placed his own mask on his misshapen face. He moved the hose into position close to the pooka girl. Havesh and Starin both moved into the tiny protective room built in the corner of the workshop and from within the room Havesh turned a red, metal wheel which connected to the tanks by way of a metal pipe. This started a hissing noise and shortly afterwards, a blood red gas started to stream out of the rubber hose. At first, nothing happened and Starin started to grow impatient. But, after a short time, black veins started to appear on the pooka's face and body. Her eyes began to bleed as the gas ate away at them and she opened her mouth as if to scream again, but she couldn't. The gas had eaten away at her lungs and she could no longer draw breath. Blood poured out of her mouth and then, she was still. She had drowned in her own blood! Her small body collapsed against her bindings and her head fell against her chest, her previously beautiful, long, black ears flopping forward, hanging down to her waist.

At the turn of another metal wheel, the gas flowed out of the workshop and back into the collection tanks, ready for use on the Allied Magiks as soon as Starin had decided when and where they would meet their end.

Starin found that he was in a much better mood after this demonstration. He picked up the crude sword and grinned at it. Finally, after all these years, his plans were ready to put into action. He could finally remove the magik scum from his planet.

"Affix the gas tanks and ensure that my army is outfitted in armour made from this metal. Nirvana, I am coming for you!"

10
A Blooming Rose

It took some time for Will to recover from the Hell's Gate Mission. He was exhausted from eight days of high stress levels and little sleep. But, after a few days of rest and good food, he was feeling much better. He had kept going to the wagon storage sheds which had become home to his engines during that time as he considered his work with the engines as therapeutic.

As he was oiling up the Darjeeling one morning, Rosa crept up and tapped him on the shoulder.

"Hey teacher," she teased.

"Hey student," he replied. "You ready to get your learn on?"

Will had already steamed Sherpa up, she just needed to be taken out of the shed, ready for Rosa's lesson. Rosa climbed into the cab and Will started showing her what each instrument did and how to use it. After stopping for lunch, Will started to drive the engine up and down the demonstration line, showing Rosa exactly how each control worked. She learned quickly and it wasn't long before she was confident enough to have a go. Rosa may have been confident, but she was also terrified! She knew what these engines meant to Will and didn't want to damage them in any way. So, her hands were shaking as she took hold of Sherpa's regulator. Rosa wasn't used to feeling this scared. She had always thrown herself into any situation with reckless enthusiasm. But her growing feelings for Will were making it harder to ignore the ball of fear that had developed in her gut.

As Rosa gripped the regulator, Will whispered quiet words of encouragement from over her shoulder. He was standing right behind her and, Rosa had to admit, his presence was comforting. Rosa reached for the whistle, gave it a toot, and then opened the regulator as she had been taught to do. Steam whooshed from the cylinders and Sherpa lurched into motion. Rosa laughed in delight as she slowly took the engine down the demonstration line. She was amazed at how quickly the engine responded to the controls and at its speed along the track. It wasn't long before she had to apply the brakes and throw the engine into to reverse to take it back to the sheds.

Rosa's lesson drew quite a few onlookers. She was still very careful to disguise who she was, but her tail made it obvious that she was a kitsune. The kitsune were usually a reserved and quiet race, and this was not what folk expected to see. It made them wonder who this new kitsune was and made some folk a little jealous, as they were fascinated by Will and his engines.

Once the pair had finished the day's instruction, Rosa threw her arms around Will in sheer delight and hugged him until he could hardly breathe. As she tried to pull away, Rosa realised that her tails, which often had minds of their own, had wrapped around Will and were holding them both tightly together. Blushing furiously, Rosa unwrapped her tails and started to give reasons for why she had to leave the shed.

"What's wrong? Rosa? What just happened?"

"I can't talk about it here. Come and find me this evening, in my garden," and at that, she was gone.

"What wasss that all about?" So'Ren asked.

"I was hoping that you would tell me!" a very confused Will replied.

Rosa had been using another cabin whilst disguised. Staying at her own home would have given her identity away so, she had moved into another, which was closer to the engine sheds. However, for this conversation, she knew that she had to be in her own garden, under the trees she had nurtured over the years. Since her "death" Rosa's mother had been tending the garden and was often seen weeding and pruning, looking for all the world like a grieving mother. Actually, Nirvana had always loved that garden and often went there if she needed time to think. She and Rosa regularly sat under the stars, discussing the events of the day. It was Nirvana's wish that Rosa would take over as leader one day, but this wasn't guaranteed. The Folk of Vitae chose their leaders. The position wasn't given as a birthright. But, during those late-night discussions, Rosa showed that she had the intelligence and compassion to be an amazing leader, even if she didn't believe it herself.

Rosa picked up some supplies and then crept into her garden. She was still embarrassed by her wayward tail and how she thought it had revealed her true feelings about Will to everyone in the engine sheds. Of course, it had also opened her own eyes to her true feelings. She had known that Will made her feel good and that she enjoyed spending time in his company, but it had taken her tail to make her realise that she loved him.

Loved him! He was a human, yet she loved him. Her mind was spinning, and she was, once again, shaking. Will had turned her into a quivering wreck and she didn't mind at all!

Rosa laid a blanket on the ground and placed her basket on it. She took her time and prepared a beautiful picnic next to the small pond, under the saku tree. The tiny, pink flowers had just started to bloom and they gave off a sweet delicate perfume. It made this spot the perfect place for tonight.

Just after sunset, Will crept into the garden. He had done his best to clean the engine muck off and make himself look presentable. Somehow, in his gut, he had known that this meeting was important. When he saw Rosa sat under the saku tree, waiting for him, his heart skipped a beat. She was stunning. He knew that there were a lot of obstacles to them having a relationship, not least was the fact that he might have to return to his own world one day. But seeing her, sat under those beautiful pink blossoms, he knew that he would never leave Vitae. His heart belonged here, with Rosa.

Will walked over and sat down next to Rosa. They smiled and chatted for some time, neither one knowing how to tell the other how they felt. Rosa started by asking Will about Sherpa; a safe subject!

"I have wanted my own engine since I was a boy but never thought it would actually happen. So, when I was offered an apprenticeship on the Ginger Line I took it. I had to move from my hometown, up to the Highlands, but it was definitely worth it. A friend was just reading a magazine one day when he saw that the Darjeeling railway had an old engine just rusting away. They weren't using it anymore. He told me and I contacted them to see if they were willing to sell it and the rest is history. When I eventually got it back to the Ginger Line, I worked on it every moment that I could. On the day that I arrived here, it had just finished its overhaul and safety checks. It had just been approved to be used on our line. That was why I couldn't leave it to explode."

"Your devotion to the engines is amazing. I love seeing you work on them and seeing how much you care about them. It is a wonderful thing to watch.

The two sat back against the tree trunk and Rosa knew that the time had come and she couldn't put this off any longer.

"Will, there is something I need to tell you," she started, almost whispering. She took a deep breath, then sighed and started "I.., when you first got here, I wasn't sure about you. Actually, I thought you were a pain in my rump! But now. Well now, I feel very differently. My feelings for you have grown over time and well, now, I realise that I...

I love you!"

Will was just staring at her, mouth open, eyes wider than a dinner plate. He didn't say anything, just stared at her.

Rosa braced herself for his reaction. Did he not feel the same way? Had she read him wrongly? What...

"Oh, thank goodness for that!" Will replied, eventually. "I thought I was going to have to tell you that I loved you and I didn't know where to start." He was grinning from ear to ear as he pulled Rosa towards him. He kissed her and her tails, once again, wrapped themselves around the two young lovers.

Hours passed before Will and Rosa packed up the remains of the picnic. They wanted to stay longer, but knew that they had to leave before daybreak. Rosa could not be seen in her garden if they were to maintain the deception of her death. Just as they were about to creep out of the garden, hand in hand, a black garbed figure, wielding a sword, leapt out from the shadows. It was Nirvana and she was holding the sword to Will's throat.

"Mother! What are you doing?"

"Silence daughter. This is between Will and me. Know this, human! Rosa is my beloved child, and I will protect her until my death, and even afterwards. If you ever hurt her, I will bury this sword into the most delicate part of your body. Do you understand?"

Will gulped, carefully! The sword was very sharp!

"I promise that I will never hurt her. I love her. Aaaand I am a bit afraid of her too. In fact, I think she would do nasty things to my delicate parts before you ever got to me, so..."

Nirvana lowered her sword and grinned at Will.

"I know. But it is my duty as a mother, to at least offer to defend my daughter's honour!"

"Mother!"

Will and Nirvana laughed out loud at Rosa's indignant look.

"Don't worry Rosa. I approve of your choice, but you took your time in expressing your feelings! I have been waiting to pull that move for days now!"

"You knew?" Rosa asked.

"Of course I did. Mothers know everything. How many times do I have to tell you that?" Nirvana was grinning at her daughter and Will couldn't help laughing.

“I have to get back to the shed and get Sherpa fired up. I will see you later.” Will leant over and kissed Rosa and then gave Nirvana a cheeky look. He gave her a peck on the cheek too and then nipped out of reach of the slap that she was aiming at his head.

“See you later too, Mother!”

Will jogged away from the garden, not quite believing his luck. He had been teleported to another world, in the middle of a conflict with humans, but had still found the woman he wanted to spend the rest of his life with.

Things were looking up!

11

DOWNFALL UNLEASHED

As if to celebrate the newly acknowledged love of Will and Rosa, all was quiet for several weeks in the City of Hope. However, the peace couldn't last and one morning a scout came to report to Nirvana. He told her of a heavily armoured, metal dragon which was manned by Starin's soldiers. Nirvana took the scout to see Will's Darjeeling, the only engine not out working that day, and asked if that was what he had seen.

"Yes, but bigger!" he replied.

This news was not good, to say the least. If Starin had engines too, the advantage that Will had given them was gone! Nirvana sent out orders for her troops to avoid this engine for now. The scout was told to find an artist who could create an image of Starin's engine and bring it straight back to the City of Hope. They needed more information before they could decide what action to take and before she would disturb Will and Rosa with this news.

Whilst Nirvana was over the moon that Rosa had found her life mate, she was also worried. If a kitsune lost their bonded mate, they often lost their desire to live. Sometimes, they went mad with rage and the desire to seek out the ultimate revenge. If Rosa lost Will in the war that was to come, Nirvana knew that she would lose Rosa too. Nirvana's own struggle after the death of her mate, Evan, had been all consuming. Only Rosa had stopped her from just fading away and she did not want that for her only child.

Nirvana also knew that the council, once they realised that Rosa was still alive, would not be happy with Rosa's choice of mate. Having Will work with them and be one of the Folk of Vitae was one thing but having him as a mate for one of the most influential people in the City of Hope, well that was another matter entirely. Nirvana knew she would have to fight that battle in the not-too-distant future.

A few days later, in the engine sheds, Will was running around, trying to get the Garratt ready to steam again. Although it had been used for the Hell's Gate rescue, the Garratt had been thought to be too big for the tracks and used vast amounts of coal. However, coal had suddenly started to be delivered at a much faster rate and quite a stockpile had developed. There had also been concern about the strength of the metal rails. The Garratt was much bigger that the other engines and there was genuine fear that it would destroy the rails, thus making any further missions impossible. The Hell's Gate rescue had alleviated some of the concerns about this, but not all. Some of the rails had had to be replaced and reinforced, but not enough progress had been made in the area around the City of Hope. What Will hadn't been told yet, was that the rails nearer to the Human cities had obviously been reinforced to take the weight of their engine. But the Garratt was still the largest engine on Vitae and the worry over the strength of the rails was great.

Will soon had the Garratt ready to go and he was pleased to find that it was running smoothly. No-one could miss the fact that Will was running the huge engine as it could be heard throughout the City of Hope; it was LOUD. It's sheer size couldn't help but impress the folk of Vitae, even though they had seen it running before. It just screamed power and might and created a sense of excitement every time it was steamed up. So, Will was not surprised when a large crowd grew up around the powerful engine. He was surprised when a huge creature walked out of the crowd and challenged him.

"I am stronger than your piece of metal. I am strongest of all on Vitae I challenge you to a test of strength. I will pull and you will pull. Whoever is the strongest will win," the creature bellowed. He was a minotaur. His huge bull-like body was muscled and toned and Will was absolutely sure that he wouldn't bet against him in a fight. However, he also knew that the mighty minotaur was no match for the Garratt.

"OK then. I accept your challenge," he replied with a grin.

A chain was attached to the coupling hook and the minotaur, Borovitch, took up the strain.

"Ready, puny creature?" the arrogant minotaur laughed.

"Ready," Will replied.

So'Ren, who was in the cab with Will, held up a green flag and the moment he dropped it the minotaur started pulling. At first nothing really happened, but gradually the massive engine started to inch forward, towards the Minotaur.

"Are you going to open the regulator any time sssoon?" So'Ren asked Will quietly.

"I don't want to embarrass him," Will joked back.

Finally, just as the crowd was starting to think that Borovitch was going to win, Will threw the regulator open and backed the engine up with ease. The crowd cheered and laughed and Borovitch joined them. No-one had actually believed that the Garratt could be beaten, but it was fun to watch Borovitch try! Borovitch then started recruiting groups to make up a tug of war team. He wanted to know how many of them it would take to beat the engine.

"I would bring my brothers to help, but we are only able to come into the City individually. We tend to cause damage if we are together!" he explained to Will, which immediately brought to mind the saying 'A bull in a china shop'.

The contest had created a party atmosphere in the City of Hope and folk started bringing picnics to the track outside the engine sheds. Will offered to cook food on the Garratt's fire and it felt just like the barbeques that the Ginger Line had held during the summer. For the first time since he had arrived on Vitae, Will felt completely at home. Rosa, disguised in her usual outfit and pretending to be a kitsune called Zaran, was sitting on the floor of the cab, with her long, shapely legs dangling over the edge of the step. She watched Will fondly and she realised that this was all she had ever wanted; Friends and loved ones gathered together, enjoying a meal and each other's company.

Whilst the barbeque was wonderful, Will and Rosa knew that, for now, there was always going to be another mission to go on and it was time to run supplies to troops in the mountain town of Griffin Peak who were defending it against Starin's forces. One of Nirvana's scouts had also reported that he had seen some strange devices being used by Starin's forces so this was the perfect opportunity to have a look at them. General Ember had placed one of his technical specialists on board the train to gather intelligence and report it back.

So'Ren and Will were concerned about this journey. The train was by far the heaviest they had ever pulled. Engineers had worked with Will to magically reinforce the couplings on the coaches and to create additional braking capabilities. Each coach had a member of the Railway Defence Force onboard and they had been trained to work the brakes in case of need. The new recruits had learnt quickly. They were keen to be of use and had spent a lot of time training with Will and So'Ren and had all volunteered to be part of this mission.

The Garratt was the only train for this mission, so it was steamed up and ready to move. In order to defend the huge engine, crossbow positions had been added to the water tank, just above the front set of driving wheels, in front of the cab. However, being defended on this journey was the least of Will's concerns. It was going to be the longest journey he had ever undertaken and he was very conscious of how vulnerable they would all be if anything happened to the engine. Will had also been told that this was a very steep track, with a sheer drop on one side. Having trained in the Highlands of Scotland, Will was used to weather, but he was still a very new driver and had never undertaken a journey of this complex nature before. Having an enclosed cab was handy if any bad weather did hit, though. The other worry was that the Garratt made a phenomenal racket, which would be amplified in the mountains. There would be no way of hiding their approach this time.

Initially, the journey went well. But, as they started the

uphill section So'Ren pointed out the storm clouds on the horizon.

"We are in for a rough night, my friend. That ssstorm is heading our way!"

"Let's pray it passes us by!"

Suddenly, they heard a massive crash of thunder which resonated around the mountains.

"I didn't think the storm was that close," Will shouted above the echo.

One of the soldiers put his head through the window of the cab.

"That wasn't like any thunder I have ever heard! I don't like this one little bit."

A short time later, the train rounded a corner, and the town came into view. Will brought the train to a halt in the makeshift station and the residents of the Griffin Peak came out to help with the unloading. The troops that had travelled up on the train supervised the unloading while Will and So'Ren remained in the cab, readying it for the journey back down to the City of Hope. The folk of Griffin Peak were not pleased to see a human at the controls of the engine, and many gave Will the filthiest of looks. He couldn't blame them, though. Starin had treated these folk so badly and as far as they were concerned, Will was just another human. So'Ren noticed how uncomfortable his friend was and gave him a reassuring wink.

As the two finished their preparations for the return journey they heard a loud volley of gunfire and the activity around the train suddenly intensified. A new sense of urgency could be felt as folk decided that it was time to leave Griffin Peak. In order to leave, Will needed to run the Garratt around to the other end of the train. He couldn't turn it around as he had originally planned as Starin's troops were in the town and no-one had expected that. Instead, he would have to reverse the engine down the mountain which was not the easiest way to drive!

Will had just finished running the engine around and coupled it up to the other end of the train when he heard a huge explosion. The shock wave nearly threw him out of the cab and he was concerned that the engine might be derailed if there were any more explosions like that. After pulling himself together he looked out of the window and up to the skyline where a red mist could be seen floating towards their position. Will couldn't take his eyes off that mist as a feeling of sheer dread filled the pit of his stomach. The gas floated over plants and animals, and then it floated over some of the town's folk. Whatever living thing that it passed died in a horrible way; coughing up blood and silently screaming in agony. The gas was poisonous.

Rosa, once again disguised as Zaran, started screaming for all the folk to get on the train. Will started ripping up some rags and coating them in coal dust. He put one around his nose and mouth and then started handing them out to the Allied Magiks troops.

"It's a gas mask. Not perfect but it will help," he yelled.

Rosa, So'Ren and the engine's defenders quickly tied the rags in place and started to fight back. They needed to give the town's folk time to get onboard. Suddenly, from out of the cloud of gas, a company of Starin's troops charged at the Allied Magik troops. Starin's soldiers were wearing proper gas masks and so were better able to attack. But that did not stop the Allied Magiks. Many created bubbles of protection around themselves and attacked with everything they had. Not all the troops had magik abilities and many of those that did lost their lives to the red gas. Once Will had the engine ready to run, he pulled out Vengance, the flintlock he had found at Hell's Gate, and started shooting at Starin's troops. It had to be said that Will was not a natural marksman and he hit very little. However, he did confuse the enemy as they had no idea what he was aiming at and what would be hit next, which was a bonus! Being inside a steel cab made him a very hard target for the enemy soldiers to hit and he took full advantage of that protection, slowing down the advance of Starin's troops long enough to allow the last of the town's folk to get onboard.

Just as they were ready to make their escape, Will heard something familiar. At first, he wasn't sure that he had actually heard the sound. There was a lot of other noise going on and it was muffled. But then, he was sure that he heard the sound of another steam engine. How that was possible, he had no idea. His was the only engine that should have been out there and no-one else was able to drive the engines back at the City of Hope. Slowly, it dawned on him. This new engine was with Starin's army. It was the only thing that made sense.

"Zaran, they have a steam engine!" he bellowed to Rosa.

He began searching the area for the engine. The red mist covered everything and seemed to distort the sound. Suddenly, though, a bright light illuminated the mist, making an eerie red glow, and out of that glow steamed an engine that Will recognised. It was an American, Baldwin tender engine and it was one that Will had seen before. He had seen it in the black and white film of a ceremony, just before it had been put on a ship, bound from America to Scotland, to showcase on the Ginger Line. But a storm had come out of nowhere and the ship, engine and all of the cargo and crew had been lost. Until now!

The Baldwin looked very different to how it had when it went onto that ship though. Its Ginger Line headboard had been removed and the whole engine had been covered in black, metallic armour. Tanks were strapped to the sides of the engine, and from those tanks poured the red gas. Many brave Allied Magiks died before the Baldwin stopped pumping the toxic fumes from its tanks. Once the tanks had emptied of their foul poison the Allied Magiks breathed a sigh of relief, however, it was short-lived. As folk tried to get closer to the Baldwin, they started screaming in agony. The Baldwin came closer and closer to the Garratt and its loaded wagons of magik-users. The closer it got, the more those passengers screamed in agony. Rosa barely managed to sprint towards the Garratt, vault into the cab and scream for Will to get the engine out of there before joining So'Ren on the floor of the cab, moaning in agony. It was all Will could do to not drop everything and go to her. To help her. To stop the pain. But, he knew that, right now, she needed him to get the Allied Magiks away from that engine as fast as he possibly could. Steam engines take time to get moving, but the Garratt had been ready to move and they had the benefit of a downhill slope to get things going more quickly. The driver of the Baldwin tried to manoeuvre it onto the run round loop and block Will's escape, but he wasn't fast enough. The Garratt steamed out of the town and down the mountain to safety. Will had been terrified that the Baldwin would follow them, but for some reason, it didn't start down the dangerous mountain track. It stopped on the outskirts of the town and didn't go any further.

On the Baldwin, the driver was staring, furiously at the departing Garratt. He didn't dare start the Baldwin down the slope after it. He just didn't have the experience to safely navigate the treacherous, unfamiliar tracks. General Watkins would be very unhappy with him, but the King would be even more angry if he damaged the War engine!

Will navigated the treacherous, unfamiliar tracks in a state of terror. He didn't have a lot of experience of driving alone, and Rosa and So'Ren weren't in any condition to help him. Gradually, though, he saw that their pain levels were dropping and they became more responsive to him.

"What the hell just happened? Did you inhale the gas?" he asked as they managed to get back on their feet.

"No. It wasn't the gas. It was that engine. Just being close to it was agony!" Rosa replied shakily. She moved in closer to Will and he put an arm around her and drew her into him.

"I wassn't out in the mist, but the pain I felt asss that engine got clossser! I have never known it's like. Sssomething on that engine iss dessigned to causse pain to Magik-usserss." So'Ren added.

Will kept the engine moving for a long time. He got So'Ren to take over as the driver so that he could work the fire. The lizard man wasn't yet up to the heavy work of wielding a fireman's shovel. Once it was clear that they had escaped the invading army, Will stopped the engine so that the passengers could take some time to recover themselves and clean off any remnants of that red gas. Many threw themselves into the mountain stream that Will had stopped alongside. The water was bitterly cold, but they were desperate to rid themselves of the fear that the gas was still on their clothing and skin.

Will took the time to fill the water tanks of the Garratt and then headed to the coaches to see if the medicas needed his help. As he walked towards the rear coaches, Will heard raised voices. Two of Griffin Peaks' former inhabitants were arguing with one of the Allied Magik troops. The brakeman, from the Railway Defence Force, saw Will heading towards them and frantically beckoned him over. Before he got there though, fists started flying and more troops piled in to try and put a stop to whatever was going on. Suddenly, Rosa was amongst them, and all activity stopped. Rosa rarely used her magik, but needed to put this fight down quickly . She wrapped each of the folk in a rope of energy which held their arms to their sides and immobilised them.

"What on Vitae is going on here?" she asked in a very quiet, dangerous voice.

Will winced. If Rosa was using a quiet voice, it meant that she was very, very angry and an angry Rosa was not much fun. Her ears were pointed downwards, and her tails spread out in a fan behind her, all bristling with anger.

Will joined Rosa, curious as to why a fight had broken out now. He avoided standing too close though. Even he was a little afraid of her at that moment!

"Zaran! I am sorry for the disturbance. Please allow me to explain, or... or show you" a very nervous soldier replied. Zaran might not have been the daughter of the leader of the Folk of Vitae, but she had still wrapped up several folk in bonds of magik and looked quite cross at that moment. The nervous soldier decided that deference was probably his best defence to the relatively unknown kitsune at that moment.

There, in the corner of the coaches, was a human, tied up and gagged. They had taken a prisoner!

"These people wanted to take him out and execute him, but... well.. He is just a child."

Will brought a lamp into the coach and realised with a jolt, that the prisoner was indeed, a child. Probably no more than 13 years of age and as thin as a stick. His cheeks were hollowed out and his uniform hung off him. He looked as if he was starving. Will walked over to the boy and helped him to stand up. He brought him out of the gloomy coach, into the clean mountain air, handing him a cup of water which the boy gulped down.

"Steady now. You will choke if you drink it too quickly. Here, eat this." Will handed the boy some of the dry biscuits he had been intending to eat on the way back to the City of Hope. This boy looked like he needed it a lot more than Will did.

The boy nervously took the food and briefly inspected it. Then he seemed to inhale it in one single breath!

"Wow! You must have been hungry, to eat that without even blinking! It isn't the best tasting thing in Vitae, is it?"

The boy looked at Will and those around him. His eyes were wild with fear, but he also seemed curious. There was a strong possibility that he had never seen anyone but other humans before.

"Don't be afraid. We won't hurt you. These people are just angry with Starin. He has hurt them for many years, and they wanted to hurt him back. But, as they are reasonable people, they know that hurting you wouldn't worry Starin in the slightest!" Will was not only speaking to the boy and the people of Griffin Peak knew it. They knew that putting this child to death would make them no better than Starin.

Rosa asked the boy a few questions, but he didn't know much. All he could tell them was that the red gas and anti-magik armour were new, but that the engine had been around for a while. He told them that he had joined the army as he was starving. He had no family and had no other way of feeding himself. There were lots of children amongst Starin's troops, all just trying to survive. There were no other facilities for orphan children in the human city.

The child was handed over to a Griffin Peaker who had a whole bevy of children with her. Will ensured that the train was quickly made ready to depart and gave a short whistle blast to tell everyone it was time to get back on board. They were all keen to get to the City of Hope and its relative safety.

As soon as they arrived Will and Rosa dashed off to report to Nirvana, leaving So'Ren to manage cleaning and oiling the Garratt. This was a fine with So'Ren. He had no desire to face Nirvana that evening. He had been through enough already!

Nirvana was horrified by the report of events at Griffin Peak.

"I had received reports of a large metal dragon and had sent scouts to investigate, but had heard nothing back yet," she declared.

"Mother! Why didn't you tell us? If we had known that there was another train-,"

"Engine" Will put in.

"-engine, sorry! We would have been better prepared. Lives could have been saved."

"Maybe, but if you had heard the rumours of another engine, you would have wanted to rush off and investigate.

I could not let you do that, so sent scouts to find more information. They have not returned yet. Stormwind and Ember were aware of this and we agreed that it was information that did not need to be shared for the present time. "

Nirvana and Rosa glared at each other. Both were angry and it wouldn't take much for an all-out shouting match to start.

"Rosa," Will started, but Rosa didn't wait to listen. She spun on her heel and stormed out.

"You should have told us." Will chided Nirvana. "We are in this together, and keeping secrets just breeds mistrust."

Nirvana sighed. "I thought I was doing the right thing. Giving the two of you time together, without the worries of Vitae on your shoulders. I was wrong and I am sorry. I will speak to her in the morning."

"Will, I have something for you. A token of appreciation for what you have done today," Nirvana said. She reached for a small package wrapped in a leather pouch and handed it to Will.

"It is an anelace and it was a gift from my father. Now, I would be honoured if you would take it."

Will unwrapped the blade from its pouch and admired the workmanship. It was a beautiful knife, held in a silver sheath and engraved with scenes of battle. The blade of the knife had the head of a dragon carved into the base, with tiny red rubies in its eyes. These glinted red as it caught the fire light. The cross-guard was in the shape of unfurled dragon's wings and its name was Fury.

"Nirvana! I can't accept this. It is too precious…"

"I want you to have it and I will not listen to your

objections," she interrupted.

Will didn't know what else to say so he threw his arms around Nirvana and hugged her tightly.

"Thank you," he whispered.

"You are welcome," she replied and with that she left the council chambers.

12
Running Repairs

The next morning, all of those exposed to the red gas and the anti-magik armour were still feeling the effects. All felt exhausted and their breathing was wheezy. The medicas had been busy all night, ensuring that there were no serious side effects and treating the injured from the battle, of which there were many. Will had been to the infirmary to see if there was anything he could do to help and had worked there for a while. The young boy that had been captured was being held in the infirmary as the medicas were concerned with how thin he was. His name was Thad and he and Will had a good chat about the City of Hope and what he would be doing there. Will had suggested that the medicas put him to work doing light duties. He didn't want Thad getting bored and causing trouble.

A little later, Will went to find So'Ren, who had spent much of the evening with him, getting the Garratt cleaned up and ready to run at short notice, if needed. Once he had finished, So'Ren had returned home, to the cabin next door to his parents' and Will found his friend there having a meal with them. So'Ren's mother, Amelie, was fretting over him and feeding him his favourite foods. She was worried about how unwell her son looked and, when Will politely knocked on the open door, she frowned at him. Will thought that Amelie blamed him for her son being unwell, but he need not have been concerned. When she realised that it was Will on the doorstep, Amelie gave a broad smile and flicked her tongue in greeting. She was fond of the young human and enjoyed having him pop round for a nice 'cuppa' as he called it.

So'Ren's father, Morpheus, was the chief blacksmith in the City of Hope and was built like a brick outhouse! He had muscles on his muscles and the biggest shoulders Will had ever seen. Their cabin sat alongside the forge where he worked and he could be heard furiously hammering on a piece of metal at that moment. Will could hear him bellowing and roaring as he worked. Something about getting his hands on King Starin and doing some very... unpleasant things to him. There was quite a lot of swearing involved too. Amelie looked embarrassed and scolded her husband through the open window. Will was always amazed at Amelie. She was only as tall as Will's shoulder and slim as a stick, but she kept Morpheus tightly under control and they obviously adored each other.

"Morpheusss! Language! We have guestsss."

"What? Oh! Ssssorry dear. Will, is that you? Good to sssee you? How are you feeling? Not too badly affected by thiss red misst? Why, if could get my hands on Starin, I would..." Morpheus started chuntering away again but soon stopped when he heard Amelie hissing at him.

Initially, Morpheus hadn't trusted Will. He saw him as the enemy and thought he was corrupting his young son. It had taken a long conversation with So'Ren to put his fears to rest. Once Morpheus had seen how excited his son was about working with these amazing machines, and once Morpheus had been to visit the engines himself, he understood that his 'young' son had grown up and was very capable of making informed decisions. Then, Will had started coming around for a visit and Amelie had decided that she was very fond of the human so Morpheus guessed he had no choice but to follow suit. He often helped So'Ren come up with new and innovative ways to improve the performance of Will's engines and had helped with the plans for converting the Sherpa to an infernoss crystal. It wouldn't be long before that engine could travel the rails without coal and Morpheus knew that would be a relief for the dwarven miners! They were working flat out, trying to keep up with the demand of the engines.

So'Ren had big plans for the engine fleet too. He wanted to create new engines and more efficient replacement parts so that, when Will's engines broke down or wore out, there would be plenty of spares and replacement engines available. The versatility of the engines was something that the Allied Magiks couldn't afford to lose. His desire to replace Will's engines was a scheme that he was not sharing with Will. So'Ren knew that the engines were what gave Will a sense of security. Having lost everything, including his world, Will was very vulnerable and often felt lost and alone in this strange place where even his species was hated. So'Ren wasn't sure that he would have fared as well as Will had, if the roles had been reversed.

Before Will's arrival, So'Ren had been a bit of an outcast. Other than Rosa, very few of the City of Hope's residents had known him, or even cared to know him. Traditionally, children followed their parents in a trade amongst the folk in the city. So'Ren, however, did not have the build to be a blacksmith. He had inherited his mother's build; slim and willowy. His mother was an artist and loved to be outdoors amongst the flora and fauna of Vitae but So'Ren wasn't interested in that either. What So'Ren loved was mathematics and creating 'things' . He loved fiddling with bits of metal and cogs and wheels, making useful implements that made folks' lives easier. He had been successful too. He had created machines that lifted heavy weights and were widely used in industrial and mining facilities. He had also created a machine to help his mother with drying the washing. Infernoss crystals were expensive and not widely available so could not be used in the homes of folk. So, So'Ren found a way to spin clothing over a fire and this made the clothing dry much more quickly. His mother loved it and had started telling her friends all about it. Others wanted a spinning dryer and So'Ren had started making them. But this had made him seem strange to the other folk and they had started avoiding him, just in case he said something that they might not understand, thus making them seem unintelligent. Rather than making him popular, So'Ren's designs made him even less popular.

Then Will had come along. Will and his amazing engines. These were the thing of dreams for So'Ren. He was fascinated with them from the very start. Despite his fear of this human, So'Ren knew he had to befriend him if he was ever going to get a really good look at what made these things work. Even more amazing was that the human, Will, seemed to know the answers to his questions. What So'Ren learnt over those first few weeks had made him see that he could be a much better engineer. Will had been amazed at how quickly the young lizard man had come to understand the inner workings of his beloved engines. Initially reluctant to allow anyone to touch his prized possessions, Will had soon accepted So'Ren's help in maintaining and, even driving, the metal dragons. Their friendship made life so much better, even if there was a war going on!

Will and So'Ren spent the rest of that morning with Amelie and Morpheus. Neither one of them felt up to a day of heavy work, so they chatted and drank tea and had mid meal before strolling back to the sheds to run a check on the engines. Both were comfortable in each others company and were so grateful to have found friendship in these troubled times.

13
A Warrior Revealed

Later in the day, Will and Rosa headed out into the forest. Rosa had said that she wanted to teach Will something about the kitsune and some of their abilities. Will was intrigued, he thought he knew Rosa well by now.

"This is going to be easier to show you, rather than try and explain." Rosa began. "Just.. don't get weird about it!"

"OK." Will was really curious now. He was looking right at Rosa and then he wasn't! In front of his very eyes, she morphed into the sleekest, most beautiful 9 tailed fox that he had ever seen. This fox wasn't like the mangy creatures that lived on the Ginger Line, scavenging for food. Oh no! This fox was larger than them, her fur was black, shiny and well groomed and matched her hair colour in her bipedal form. She still had the most piercing green eyes, but she was a fox. A fox! With four legs, 9 tails and a wet nose. It was hard not to get weird!

"I... err... I...wow! Trying not to be weird here but... Wow! You are gorgeous! Can I stroke your fur?"

In his mind, Will heard Rosa laughing. "If you want!"

"Oh! And you are telepathic. Obviously!" Will remarked

ironically. "This is a lot!"

"Are you alright?" Rosa asked in his mind. "Do you want me to change back?"

"God, no! Stay just as you are. I could look at you like this all day!"

Rosa came up to Will's legs and rubbed along them. Then she rose up on her back legs and put her front paws on his shoulder. She gave his ear a quick lick and then leapt off into the forest. Rosa was graceful as a two-legged creature, but in this form she was even more so. Will was staggered by her sinuous movements and her stealthiness.

"It is time to hunt," she sent and then she was gone. In what seemed like a flash, she was back with a small creature, like a rabbit, hanging from her jaws.

Rosa quickly changed form and sat next to Will.

"Are you OK?" she asked again.

Will realised that she was scared of his reaction. Did she think that he wouldn't love her anymore? But that was mad and the wrong way around. How could SHE love HIM?

"I am more than OK! I knew you were amazing, but now, you are phenomenal. I, you, aaggghh. I feel so inadequate. You are this amazing, magik, mystical being and I am just... well, just me. What can you possibly see in me?"

"I love you and that is enough. You are kind and caring. You are intelligent... most of the time! You listen to what I have to say and you get on with my mother!"

At that, they both laughed and the fear passed. They loved each other and that was enough.

"Now. Let me teach you how to hunt." Rosa spent the rest of the day teaching Will how to catch his own food and what to do with it once he had caught it. They had a delicious lunch, cooked over a fire and sat in a peaceful glade. As they were sitting chatting, most of Rosa went very, very still. Only her ears moved.

"Stay here!" she whispered.

Will made to ask her what was going on, but she placed a finger on his lips and signed for him to watch. Then she was gone. A second later she streaked across the glade in her fox form. From off to his right, Will caught a movement in the undergrowth. There standing as still as a statue, was a huge wild boar. Its beady eyes were scanning the glade and its nose was twitching this way and that, trying to figure out what the strange scent was. Then, in the blink of an eye, it started to charge towards Will. How an animal that bulky could move that quickly, Will would never know, but it seemed to cross the glade in an instant. He didn't even have time to react to his imminent goring, or feel sad that he would be leaving Rosa when he had only just found her.

She was there in an instant, pouncing on the boar mid-flight. The fight was short and gory, with Rosa ripping chunks out of the boar. She moved like the wind and, fast as the animal was, the boar just couldn't keep up. Eventually, Rosa tore its throat out with her sharp teeth. The boar hadn't even come close to injuring Rosa. When she got back to Will, she was panting with exertion and covered in boar's blood. She checked that Will was unhurt and then settled down to clean her fur.

"Well, that was fun!" Will commented. Rosa tipped her ears at him and kept on cleaning.

When Rosa had finished, she changed back into her two-legged form and together they dragged the immense carcass back to the City. They drew quite a crowd of traders who were all trying to buy meat, hide or horns. Rosa negotiated like a pro and they ended up walking back to the engine sheds a lot better off than when they had left to hunt earlier in the day.

That evening the two sat next to a roaring fire back in the glade where they had hunted earlier in the day. They had cooked, and eaten, two huge steaks, and had settled down under the stars to discuss the world and the situation they found themselves in. Will talked of his home in Scotland, and how he wished he could let his friends know that he was safe and well. He was also worried about the damage that the explosion would have done to the Ginger Line and how it would cope without the three engines which had been hurled into Vitae with him.

Rosa talked of her desire to protect her people and of the pressure she felt to follow in her mother's footsteps. She did not feel up to the task of being the leader of the council. How could she possibly live up to her mother's expectations? Will didn't mention that he thought she would be amazing as the leader and that she naturally took the role whenever her mother was not around. He knew she would be a fantastic leader, but hopefully not for many, many years yet.

They had just fallen silent and were enjoying the feeling of being pleasantly full and warm when a twig snapped at the edge of the clearing. Rosa was on her feet in an instant, and Will quickly followed.

"What is it?" he asked.

"I don't know yet? It's an animal of some sort, but nothing should approach the fire though, so we should be safe enough. There! " she pointed suddenly. Will searched the trees where Rosa had pointed and after a moment, saw a pair of red eyes staring back at him, then he saw another and another.

"Rosa?"

"I know, I see them too. What are they doing here?" she asked.

"Are you asking me?"

"What? No! Of course not! But they shouldn't be here at all. There haven't been forest leon's in this region for generations. They were hunted to extinction by the humans. The fire should stop them from attacking, but be prepared, just in case."

Rosa drew Firebringer and moved to a fighting stance. Will's musket was beside his blanket, on the ground, and whilst it was loaded, it only fired one round before needing to be reloaded and that would take time. So, he drew his anelace.

Suddenly, the biggest of the leons leapt towards Rosa. She moved to block and started the dance of the fight. Will didn't have the chance to watch for long. Another huge leon came into the clearing and made for Will. All of the training that he had done with Rosa came into his mind. He automatically dropped into a fighting crouch and, when the leon attacked, he fought back. The leon fell to Fury's blade in a matter of moments. As the next leon approached, Will saw Rosa fall from the corner of his eye. She was facing numerous leons, including the mighty alpha. Will saw her head hit the floor and something inside him snapped. He had never been a natural fighter, but that was probably because he was a natural healer; he preserved life, he didn't take life. But seeing his beloved Rosa, hurt and bleeding was more than he could take. He had read of Berserkers, and that is what he became now. He was not consciously in control of his body and his vision had turned red. His movements were those of a seasoned warrior and before he knew what was happening, the alpha leon lay dead on the floor, with Fury buried up to the wings in his chest.

"Will! Will, you can stop now. They are gone. Will? Can you hear me?" Rosa called weakly to him.

Suddenly, his vision cleared and he could see a very pale Rosa, lying on the ground with blood pouring down her cheek. He ran over to her and checked her injuries. He stopped the bleeding and covered the head wound with a clean napkin from their picnic. She was not badly hurt, but had been knocked out for a moment and couldn't focus her eyes properly. She needed to be checked over by the medicas as quickly as possible.

"What happened to you Will? You fought as if you had held that blade all of your life." Rosa asked weakly.

"I... I... don't know. I just saw you go down and I needed to get to you, to protect you. But, the leon was in the way. And then he wasn't. I.. don't remember anything else." Will was very uncomfortable with what he had just done but knew that he had done it for the right reasons. His love for Rosa had completely overwhelmed his usual quiet, nurturing nature and turned him into a raging beast. He was glad for that, but also scared.

He gathered their belongings together and put them up in a tree for safety. Then he picked Rosa up and carried her back into the city. As he rushed through the streets, crowds of onlookers gathered and slowed his progress. Will could feel himself getting angrier and angrier until he thought he would explode. Just as he was about to start screaming he heard Nirvana shout “MOVE ASIDE” and it was like waves parting. Will charged through the gap and into the cool, open space of the infirmary.

“Will, what is going on?” Nirvana demanded, taking Rosa’s hand in hers.

“I am fine. There was a forest leon pack in the glade. They attacked despite the fire!” Rosa replied.

Will placed Rosa onto the examination table and was then ushered out by the medicas. He and Nirvana went to a waiting room and Will filled her in on everything that had happened that evening, including how he had completely lost his mind when he saw Rosa go down.

“It’s called a Warriors’ Bond.” Nirvana told him. “It usually only happens when one member of a bonded pair of kitsune face a deadly peril. The other goes into a frenzy in order to protect their mate. They develop faster reaction speeds, enhanced strength and abilities until the danger has passed, or until they are defeated. I do not know why this has happened; you are not a kitsune, so it should not have been possible.”

Once the medicas had checked Rosa over and made sure that she wasn’t badly hurt, Will and Nirvana went in to see her. She was not happy at having to stay at the infirmary overnight and she was making that fact very well known! After a short visit, Will and Nirvana were ordered to leave so that the patient could get some rest and Will was happy to comply. A grumpy Rosa was not a fun experience!

14
ALCO ESCAPE

King Starin had called a high-level meeting at his stronghold in the capital city, Stronghelm. He was celebrating the unparalleled success that they had achieved at Griffin Peak. Despite the escape of many of the Allied Magiks, the townsfolk and the human and his engines, Starin's forces had dealt a mighty blow to their enemy. The red gas and anti-magik armour had been a resounding success. They had also captured large numbers of Griffin Peak's population and tests were currently being conducted on those with magik, to see if they could make the red gas any more effective.

"This may have been a successful mission, but I want more. That armour should be deadly to the magik scum. I don't just want them to have a headache! I want them screaming in agony, just before they die!" he had laughed.

The Generals present thought that this was a great plan and started discussing other ways to make the Allied Magiks suffer.

Not all of those present were enjoying Starin's joke. Prince Steele had been struggling to understand his father's hatred of the Allied Magiks for many years. When he was younger, he had assumed that he was missing something, but now, he knew that he could never understand his father's hatred. Steele could not comprehend that hatred and hoped that he was never able to feel that amount of animosity towards anyone. The Generals that followed Starin were just evil; hanging onto the coattails of their deranged king. Starin gave them the perfect outlet for their cruel, psychopathic tendencies.

Steele had had enough. He sat in the meeting and realised that his father needed to be stopped and Steele knew that he couldn't do that from within this castle. He would have to get out and find the Allied Magiks. Whilst the rest of the attendees dreamt up new and better ways to inflict pain on the magik-users, Steele came up with possible escape plans. This wasn't the first time he had thought about leaving, but this time he was certain. He knew that getting out of the castle was the right thing to do, but he worried about leaving the people within its walls. There was one that he absolutely would not leave without and that was his maid, Ebunnie. Ebunnie was a pooka. She, and her family, had been at the castle for most of her life as her mother had been captured by Starin's forces and not allowed to leave. She had been maid to Prince Steele since his mother had left and, as they were of similar ages, they had become friends. Servants didn't get a lot of time off in Starin's castle, which had meant that their time together had been limited when they first met. But Steele had realised that if Ebunnie got her chores done more quickly, she would have more time to be with him and she would get time to rest, another thing servants weren't allowed to do much of. Steele had started to clean out the fireplace and tidy his chambers. He saved food from his meals and the two of them often sat together eating and reading a book, playing a card game or just talking. These times were the best of his life and the two had quickly fallen in love. Ebunnie was his whole world. She completed him and he would protect her, even if it meant his death.

Leaving his father was an easier decision. Steele and Starin did not get on! But, Steele still worried about the king. He wished that Starin was a better man, or that he could be redeemed, but being at that meeting and listening to him laugh at the pain and suffering of others was the last straw. He had planned an escape many times before, but this time he knew he had to go through with it.

When the celebrations had progressed to the point where Steele felt that he wouldn't be missed, he left the hall and made his way to his chambers and sent word for his maid to attend him. Steele found a small travel bag and packed a few items of clothing and personal belongings. He didn't have much as his father wouldn't allow superfluous objects, but he did have a small statue that his mother had smuggled in to him and a few books and trinkets.

After a few short minutes a knock came at his door and Ebunnie entered the room. He quickly told her of his fathers behaviour and of the plan to leave the city. After checking that she wanted to leave with him he advised her to pack a small bag and to be back in his room at nightfall. They would go out under cover of darkness.

Ebunnie was stunned by Steele's decision. At first, she thought he was joking, but she knew how much he hated his father's cruel ways. However, this was not an easy decision and she had not replied to Steele immediately. Her mother was still in the castle and leaving her would be hard.

Ebunnie's sister had disappeared several weeks earlier and no-one knew where she was, or if she was even alive. But Ebunnie also knew that her mother would want her to be free and to spend her days with the man she loved. After checking that he was sure he knew what he was doing, Ebunnie finally agreed to leave and they put together a very quick plan. Being the king's son did give Steele some knowledge that others didn't have. The king had never really trusted his son with much, but there were a few small details which gave them an edge. He knew that there would be a steam train, sat on the tracks, ready to go to collect supplies from the harbour. Steele had received a few driving lessons from the train's crew without his fathers knowledge. Starin didn't let anyone near his prized possession. So Steele had a very basic understanding of how it worked. He could just about run it.

Shortly after nightfall, Steele and Ebunnie walked confidently through the halls of the castle. The king and his generals were still celebrating in the grand audience hall and most of the domestic staff were concerned with keeping the men happy. Starin was known for his temper and so, the staff had to work hard to ensure nothing went wrong. Steele knew that creeping would make the two of them stick out like a sore thumb, and besides, he was the prince. He had every right to be wandering around the halls at night. After what seemed like an eternity, they arrived at the doors which were closest to the engine's siding. Steele was very conscious that Havesh's lab was just beyond the engine, and he did not want the crazy old man interfering in their escape. They were in luck though. The engine's crew were not in the cab, they were in the shed, gathering their gear. Ebunnie scrambled up the ladder and Steele quickly followed. Once inside, they found that the engine was steamed up and ready to go, which was their second bit of good luck. It was almost as if the universe wanted them to escape. But then...

"Oi, who is in the cab? Get out! I will call the guard!"

"Steele, we need to leave. Now!" Ebunnie squeaked.

"I know, I know. Let me just... hold on." The engine lurched as Steele opened the regulator and released the brakes.

The engine had started moving down the tracks and was quickly building up speed. From behind them came shouts from the engine's crew and then the sound of muskets firing and then metal striking metal! Steele pushed Ebunnie to the ground as they sped towards the city gates and through them, towards the forest, and freedom.

Once they were clear of the city, Ebunnie gave a joyous cry. She had not left since her capture and the sense of relief was overwhelming. With tears streaming down her face, she leapt up and hugged Steele.

"Thank you, thank you, thank you."

"You are welcome, but we aren't out of the woods yet!" he laughed. "I have no idea where we are going or how much fuel we have on board. I didn't get much time to plan this escape!"

The engine, an Alco which had mysteriously arrived at the same time as the War Engine, continued on for a few hours before Steele needed to stop for water. They had just filled the tank and were preparing to leave when Ebunnie thought she heard a noise. Steele couldn't hear anything over the sound of the engine, but he trusted Ebunnie's intuition. Suddenly, she realised that the noise she was hearing was the sound of horses hooves; lots of horses hooves!

"He sent the cavalry after us. Of course he did. Why am I surprised?" Steele groaned.

They leapt up and into the cab and tried to start the engine moving again. This time though, their luck failed them. The engine didn't move, and Steele couldn't see what the problem was. He looked over at Ebunnie, with regret in his eyes. Then he jumped down from the cab and drew his sword.

"Run! They may not know you are with me. I can die happier knowing that you are free. Run!"

"No, I won't leave you," Ebunnie cried.

There wasn't time for a debate. From out of the darkness came the shrill whistle of another steam engine. At first, Steele thought his father had sent the War Engine after them, but that would have been impossible. It took time to get an engine going from a cold start and they hadn't had time for that. Which could only mean that the whistle was from one of the Allied Magik's engines. Hope sprang up in Steele's heart. Maybe he could get Ebunnie to safety after all. He knew that his life was over, but hers could be saved.

When the engine arrived, it was actually two engines with a coach sandwiched between them. As the driver of the lead engine saw the Alco sat in the clearing, he slammed on his brakes and an almighty squealing accompanied the sound of shouting from the cab. Number 4 stopped less than a hand width from the buffers of the Alco and Steele let out the breath that he hadn't realised he was holding. To his dismay, from the cab came a HUMAN. Ebunnie hadn't been saved then. Steele turned to face the human, with his sword drawn and fully expecting to have to fight for their lives. The human cautiously approached Steele and Ebunnie.

"I think that is Will Thorpe." Ebunnie whispered. "He is the human working with my folk. The one I told you about. There have been stories about him saving folk from your father's army."

Steele remembered the stories. They had given him some hope that the fighting between Ebunnies folk and his could end one day. If a human was working with the Allied Magiks, maybe there was a chance of peace.

"Are you Will Thorpe?" Steele asked him.

"Yes. How did you know that? We haven't met, have we?"

"No but Ebunnie has heard of you. I am Prince Steele. Ebunnie and I have escaped from my father's castle. We are refugees and the cavalry are coming to get us. Will you help us? The engine won't move. I don't know what is wrong with it." Steele blurted this all out without even stopping for breath. He felt like a small child begging not to be punished, but he knew they needed this man to help them, or all was lost.

Will stared at Steele and then made a quick decision.

"So'Ren, ease her forward. Gently does it. That's it."

Will coupled Number 4 to the Alco and then told Steele and Ebunnie to get onboard, with a warning not to do anything stupid. He told one of the guards, who had followed him from No.4, to watch them and then he sprinted to the Darjeeling which was coupled to the other end of the carriage. He blasted Sherpa's whistle three times and then started the whole train slowly moving backwards out of the clearing. Just as the train pulled away and picked up speed, the cavalry charged into the clearing. General Watkins, who was leading the charge, swore loudly, ordered the halt and turned his troops around. He knew that the Prince was out of his reach for now. He wasn't going to be the one that told the King he had failed though. They would camp for the night and then move on in the morning. He would find the city of the magik scum and he would destroy it. Then he would drag the Prince out of there, dead or alive.

On the Alco, Ebunnie was hopping up and down in delight. They had escaped and they were on their way to the city of her folk. She would be safe and she would have her beloved Steele with her.

Steele wasn't feeling so confident though. The fact that Will was part of the Allied Magik's army had given him a little hope that he wasn't going to be executed as a war criminal, but he knew that he was still in a lot of danger. He didn't want to ruin Ebunnie's homecoming though. So, he plastered a smile on his face and hoped for the best.

"Control what you can control, Steele. Leave the rest to the universe,"." he told himself.

A few hours later, the train arrived back at the City of Hope. The plan had been to take Steele to the council building so that Nirvana could make a decision about what they should do with Steele. However, somehow, the residents of the City had been told who was onboard the train and a huge, angry, crowd had formed along the tracks.

"How did they know who was onboard?" Will asked So'Ren.

"Telepathy I guesssss." he replied flippantly. Then he saw Will's confused look and explained that a lot of the Allied Magiks had the ability to communicate via telepathy. Someone had obviously 'called ahead'.

Fortunately, Nirvana had been made aware and had deployed some of the Railway Defence Force to defend Will and his team, and the prisoners. Nirvana was a little conflicted though. She could completely understand why her folk were so angry. Starin had caused untold misery to the folk of Vitae and to have his son come into their city, their safe haven, was hard. But, she also knew that, if they didn't take the first steps towards a better future, it would never happen. Will had taught her that. So, she stood on the steps of the council building and addressed the furious crowd.

"Folk of Vitae! Why have you gathered in this way? What is it that you want to achieve here? Is it that you want to kill Prince Steele and his beloved? Do you want revenge on the father by punishing the son for all the evil he has committed?"

At this the crowd roared. They were angry and, yes, they wanted blood. Or at least they thought they did. At heart, the folk of Vitae were a peaceful folk. It was Starin, and his predecessors who had forced them to become battle-ready. Because of them, they had put aside their love of hearth and home and a peaceful life, in order to protect those homes and the ones they loved.

"I understand your anger. I really do. It burns in my blood too. I have lost those I love to Starin and his kin. We have all heard of the horrors of Hell's Gate and of the way our folk were treated there. But would killing Steele diminsh that horror? If we behave in this way, we are no better than the humans Starin commands. If we don't start to bring peace to Vitae, do you think Starin will? No! He will not stop until all magiks are dead. We need to take control of this war and put an end to Starin's tyranny. We can make a start by finding a way to put an end to this reign of terror.

I find myself wondering why Steele is here. Why he has left the safety of his father's castle. Wouldn't you like to know that too? Let the council meet and question Steele. We will find the truth and then we can decide what to do with him."

As Nirvana had spoken, the crowd had quietened, and their fury had eased somewhat. Those who had been rescued from Hell's Gate were having the hardest time with allowing Steele to be left unhurt. They wanted to rip him limb from limb, but they heard Nirvana and held themselves back. For the moment.

Will and So'Ren had managed to make their way back to the cab of Number 4 and they helped Steele and Ebunnie down. A large group of Hell's Gaters were hovering around the engine and glaring at the newcomers. For a moment it looked like they would ignore Nirvana and attack, but they trusted Will and they knew that he had their best interests at heart.

"Come on lads. This isn't the way. We are better than this," he quietly urged. Will turned to the brawny dwarf who seemed to be leading the hostile group. His name was Greem and he had a livid red scar running from his right eye, down to the middle of his chin. This was a momento of the time he had spent in the concentration camp. Will could see the anger in Greem's eyes, and he understood that anger, but he also knew that this fiery red-bearded dwarf had a good soul and would regret attacking Steele if he let his temper get the better of him.

"Greem, I see your anger. I see your pain. I feel that burning desire for vengeance. But think, this is the King's son! The knowledge he has will be invaluable to us."

"May I speak?" Steele asked calmly. At a nod from Will, he continued. "My father is a brutal lunatic, and I am sorry that you have suffered at his hands. He is served by evil men who do his bidding happily and enjoy causing pain. Their behaviour is abhorrent to me and if there is anything I can do to help remove his power over our world, I will do it. If there is any information that I have that will aid your fight, I will give it. If I have nothing that will help, then I will willingly fight on the front lines to take out as many of these evil doers as I can before I die. On this you have my word."

As Steele spoke, the light in Greem's eyes changed. Now, instead of fury there was a small glimmer of hope. Could this human really help them to defeat Starin? Would he? There was also suspicion in Greem's stare, but the hope gave him a reason to back down and to let Will, So'Ren, Ebunnie and Steele pass through the crowd and on into the council chambers. There he was taken into custody and told that he would be interrogated for any information he might have. Ebunnie wept and wailed at this news, but Nirvana had her swiftly taken away. She too would be questioned for anything useful she might know

Once the council meeting was over, Will and So'Ren went to take a look at the Alco. They made notes of what needed doing to the engine and then headed off to their homes. They knew that the next day would be a busy one and hoped that the information Steele had would be enough to end this war much sooner.

Meanwhile, General Watkins had sent a messenger to the King advising him that he was close to finding the City of Hope and that the Prince had taken refuge in the city.

Initially, Starin was angry at the general for not bringing his son back, but the news that the City of Hope would soon be theirs was music to his ears. Then he would be able to rid Vitae of the magik scum, forever.

15
A New Comrade

Prince Steele was not enjoying his time at the City of Hope! Despite telling the Council that he was happy to give them information about his father's army, they had decided to imprison him and question him for any other information he might have. As the son of the King, they believed that Steele would have attended all of the high-level meetings and, despite Steele and Ebunnie trying to tell them this wasn't the case, the Council insisted that the interrogation continue.

Ebunnie tried everything she knew of to get in to see Steele and to have the interrogation stopped. She cried, she screamed and she begged, but nothing would change their minds. In the end she threatened. If she was not allowed to see Steele she would ensure that the secret of the shield that surrounded the City was passed on to Starin. She knew that Starin's army would be looking for Steele and it wouldn't be difficult for her to leave the city and take the information to them. The Council were astonished that Ebunnie would go that far, but Nirvana stood and faced Ebunnie.

"Child, have you heart-bonded with Steele?"

There was silence in the chamber.

"Yes" came the whispered reply.

"Aaahh. I see. Well, that changes things." Nirvana nodded.

The council members were stunned by this information. As far as they were aware, no human had ever been heart-bonded to one of the folk. It just wasn't done. The only reason Nirvana had suspected was her daughter's relationship with Will and the council weren't aware of that as most of them thought Rosa was dead. Nirvana waited for the astonished council members to regain some composure and then turned to face Ember.

"Ebunnie will be allowed to see the Prince and they will be given quarters in the town. A guard will be placed on Steele at all times and the questioning will continue. But, as a bonded mate of one of our folk, he is to be treated as one of the Folk of Vitae. Is that clear?"

There was a lot of grumbling, but in the end the General nodded.

The first Will knew of any of this was when he saw a very bruised and battered looking Steele being led to a cabin near to the barracks of the defence force. He went over to speak to the Prince and was shocked to see the condition he was in.

"What happened to you?" he asked.

"I tripped in the sauna," he replied sarcastically.

"You have saunas here? Ha. I didn't know that!" Will responded. "What did you expect? I guess years of torture and war will make folk a little angry. Still, I didn't expect them to treat you like this"

"I didn't expect any different, and this was just one person losing their temper. I have mostly been treated well. But it is hard on Ebunnie. I hate to see her so hurt by the actions of her folk."

"You love her, don't you?"

"We are heart-bonded." Steele looked as though he was waiting for Will to attack him for some reason.

"I don't know what that means. I haven't been on Vitae that long."

Before Steele could explain, Rosa, in her Zaran disguise, came over to the pair. She had been ordered to take things easy after the Leon attack. Although she hadn't been badly hurt, her wounds needed time to heal and she had lost a lot of blood. This had meant that Rosa had been in a bad mood for days! So, Will took a deep breath and prepared himself for being patient.

"Morning Zaran. You are looking well this morning."

As soon as the words left Will's mouth, he knew that he made a mistake. He hastily added "as you do every morning." In the hope that it would redeem him. Rosa glared at him for a good 5 seconds before turning on her heel and stalking away. Will was shocked that Rosa was still angry at having had to stay in the infirmerie. He knew that she had felt weak and useless whilst in there, but her bad mood had gone on for far too long now.

"Who was that and what on Vitae did you do to upset her that much? Or does she hate you all the time?" Steele asked with a look of awe on his face.

It was Will's turn to glare this time. Then he too stalked off, nodding at the guard as he left.

During Steele's interrogation, he had given a lot of useful information. He may not have been part of the king's inner circle, but he was a very curious man and had seen many of the king's plans by rooting through his study after dark and by finding fantastic places to eavesdrop on the meetings the king had with his lunatic advisors. He knew of a few of the kings new weapons, including bolt action rifles and a ship that could fly by being attached to a balloon. This information worried the council greatly. If Starin had access to this kind of weaponry the Allied Magiks could easily lose this war. They needed to find a way to defeat Starin before he could use these weapons of hell.

Council meetings were held daily and Will was expected to attend. It took all of his negotiation skills to have Nirvana agree that he only had to attend twice a week. Training of the Defence Force was going well, but not well enough that he could afford to spend half of his days in a room full of arguing people. It was at one of these meetings that the subject of what to do with Steele now that they had finished questioning him was raised. Some wanted him put to death, but not many. Now that they knew of the heart-bond between Ebunnie and Steele, there was little desire to cause the pain that would come from breaking the bond. Will still didn't know what a heart-bond was, but Rosa had been in such a bad mood recently that he hadn't wanted to ask her. As the discussion had grown more heated, Ember suggested that Steele join the Railway Defence Force. That stopped that noise for a moment.

"Now that is a great idea," Nirvana agreed. "That way, Will can keep an eye on Steele and he can't do that much damage when he is working on the engines."

"Hang on a minute. Why do I have to take care of him? Don't you think I have enough to do, training the new team members I already have? There is also the fact that most of my trainees are the folk who have been hurt the most by

Steele's father. How are they going to feel, having to work with him every day?"

"I would imagine that they will enjoy giving him all of the worst jobs there are to do," Nirvana answered slyly.

Will wasn't happy. The real reason for his dislike of this idea was the danger that it put Rosa in. Until now, her disguise had worked and no-one had realised that she was actually Rosa. Now that Steele was in the city though, it was going to be even harder to maintain the ruse. Of course, he couldn't say that in the council chambers as most of the members were unaware that Rosa was still alive. Will didn't trust Steele and he certainly didn't want him around Rosa, asking too many questions.

So, Steele came to work for Will. And Will made him work. He had expected Steele to complain about all the dirty jobs he was assigned, but he didn't. Steele merely nodded and then got on with the task. Will had to admit that the prince was a great worker. Nothing was too much trouble, and the results were always of a high standard. But many of the Defence Force were still angry at Steele being forced on them. His father was the cause of their pain and loss and here he was, working with them. It was all Will could do to stop them from leaving the Defence Force and there were several occasions when Will had to administer first aid after a scuffle broke out. But slowly, over several weeks, his hard work and complete acceptance of his father's guilt, led the rest of Will's team to start accepting Steele.

Even more amazing was that, over the course of those weeks, Will found that he liked Steele. He was still wary of the prince, but Will appreciated his hard work and his quiet sense of humour. He knew that, if they had met in Scotland, they would have been firm friends. But they didn't meet in Scotland and Will knew that he had to maintain a distance or be in danger of revealing too many of the folk's secrets.

16
The Last Stand

Several days had passed when Steele was quietly working in the engine sheds. Will and So'Ren were tinkering with Sherpa, trying to figure out the best way to update the engine so that it would use less coal, but travel farther. This would tide the engine over until it could be converted to run on infernoss crystals.

Curious, Steele wandered over to join them to see what they were doing. He had spent quite a lot of time watching Havesh's team work on the Alco and the War Engine and so the banter and playfulness between Will and So'Ren made him feel strangely at home. Steele wasn't particularly mechanically-minded but he could follow most of what they were saying. Of course, he didn't know anything about magik or infernoss crystals, but he could remember his grandfather having similar conversations with his engineers back when Steele was just a young child. He mentioned this to Will and So'Ren.

"How long have the engines been here then?" Will asked.

"I am not sure exactly when they appeared, but they were on a transport ship which ran aground on the coast during my great grandfather's reign. He didn't do much with them, but my grandfather was fascinated with them and had a team of engineers working on them at all times, trying to figure out how they worked and what they could do. The ship had all sorts of things on it, I am told. I believe that is where our weapons came from."

"It probably is. These engines went missing from my world in the last century. That ship had been carrying weapons which had been used in a war. The ship was thought to have disappeared in, what we call, the Bermuda Triangle. Many vessels have disappeared there and it is one of the great mysteries on my world."

Will's brain was whirring. How did the ship get here? Was the Bermuda Triangle legend real and if so, was this where the vessels ended up? If that was the case, where were the crews of those vessels? One other question kept popping into Will's mind. If the Bermuda Triangle was the reason for the engines arriving on Vitae, how had he got there? Will had been nowhere near Bermuda when he had been thrown on to Vitae!

Later that day, Will and So'Ren told Nirvana and Rosa of everything they had learned from Steele. Will's mind was still spinning and full of questions, but try as they might, nobody could answer those questions.

The four of them stayed up, talking and throwing ideas into the night air, but mainly just enjoying each others company. Nirvana had mellowed so much since the fight with the forest leons and she was often found with Will, Rosa and So'Ren in evenings. Rosa had confided in Will that she and her mother had never had a particularly close relationship. Whilst they loved each other fiercely, Nirvana had always been driven and had little time to spend with her daughter. When they were together, Nirvana was training Rosa to take over her role; a role that Rosa wasn't sure she wanted. But, kitsune were born leaders and it was expected that one would take over from Nirvana. Kitsune weren't numerous. The group that Will had met on his first day on Vitae was made up of over half of all the kitsune alive. Rosa, or Zaran, was the only real choice to be the leader of the Council and this yolk weighed heavily on her shoulders. However, the days that she had spent with her mother and Will were such a blessing to her and Rosa was loving getting to know the more relaxed version of Nirvana. They were often seen giggling together when they thought no-one was looking!

Will had found the time to ask Rosa about the heart-bond and she had been amazed that he didn't know anything about it.

"But Will, when you fought the leons, did you not realise that we had bonded? That was why you were able to defeat them as you did. When we spent the night together in my garden, did you not feel the bond forming?"

"I … knew I felt different. I knew I felt closer to you and that to leave you would kill me, but I just thought that was love. Wait a minute, I feel your emotions, don't I? I have always been intuitive and am told that I am an empath so feel the emotions and moods of others, but it was so much stronger with you. Is that what the heart-bond is?"

"Yes, and that would explain it. Empaths are used to feeling what others feel and so the bond wouldn't have been so … well dramatic I suppose. We are already bonded Will. When one of us hurts, so does the other. I am sorry. I thought you knew."

"I didn't, but I love it and I love you. Anything that brings us closer together is a wonderful thing, as far as I am concerned."

Rosa looked relieved and Will went round for days with a silly grin on his face. He took time to focus on Rosa and her feelings and was amazed that he had not realised how "loudly" her heart spoke to his.

That evening, sat by the fire, everything seemed good with their world. That was until the peace was shattered by the sound of shouting and running feet coming closer and closer to their fire. Nirvana and Rosa leapt up, with a grace which still stunned Will. He and So'Ren quickly joined them, to see what was happening.

One of the scouts ran into the garden and headed straight for Nirvana.

"Forgive me, but this is urgent. There is a human at the gate, demanding to see Will and... and Rosa. I am sorry Ma'am. He says his name is Owen Trelisker?"

"Let him in," Nirvana responded, briskly.

Shortly afterwards the familiar face of Owen appeared, along with a small group of human soldiers, most of whom Will and Rosa recognised as those they had released at the battle of Sea Town.

"Owen. What are you doing here?" Will asked. The boy looked haggard and seemed to have aged a decade in the short time since they had first met. His short sandy hair was ruffled and he had black smudges under his eyes which spoke of how long it had been since he had slept well.

"I came to warn you. All of Starin's army is on its way here. The War Engine is coming too, and it is carrying the red gas. You need to be ready. They will be here before nightfall in two days." Owen then sank to the floor, exhausted.

After a moment of complete silence, Nirvana and Ember started issuing orders and getting folk moving. There was so much that needed to be done and very little time in which to do it. Will and Rosa took Owen and the other soldiers, who had arrived with him, to the medicas and then went to the sheds to ensure everything was ready for the attack. The Council had known that an attack by Starin was a possibility and that, one day, they would find the City of Hope, and plans had been put in place for when that day came. Now, it was just a case of putting those plans into action.

Will was surprised at how good he was feeling. There was going to be a war and he felt relieved! He played with the feeling in his mind, to try and work out what was going on. He suddenly realised that his intuition about Owen had been right. Will had taken a chance on Owen back at Sea Town and that chance had now paid off. They had been given warning of the imminent attack and had the time to prepare for it.

Will and Rosa went to pick Owen up from the infirmary, before heading off for the latest council meeting but he had already left so that he could give the Council as much information as he could about Starin's troops and his plan of attack. Rosa and Will left the medicas with a promise to return Owen to their ministration once they were finished and headed off to the council chambers. Nirvana, and the Council members, had barely left the chambers since Owen had delivered his disturbing report. Even with a plan in place, there was still a lot to do. At their best guess, the bulk of Starin's army would arrive in two days' time. Thanks to his bravery, Owen Trelisker had given them two days to prepare the City of Hope for this invasion and that time would save many, many lives.

"Ah Will. The very person I wanted to talk to." Nirvana declared before they even had a chance to clear the threshold. "I am going to need your trains to pull as many carriages as they can. We need to be able to evacuate those who cannot fight. How long will you need to get them ready?"

Will already knew all of this, but he also knew that Nirvana needed to ensure that he had everything prepared.

"They are as ready as they can be. I just need to fire them up. It would usually take a few hours to get the water hot enough, but So'Ren has come up with a way to get the water heated in less than one hour. You tell me when you want me to leave, and I will be ready." Will turned to the council and explained that So'Ren had been working with some of his fellow lizard folk to come up with a way to get the engines running quickly, from a cold start. It hadn't been easy as, if it was done too quickly, the boiler would be damaged and there was, currently, no way to replace it. Finally, the fire-breathing lizards had come up with the solution. Firstly, they superheated fire crystals and then placed them into the full water tank. Then the engine was fired up as usual. By using water that was already heated, it reduced the preparation time dramatically. Instead of taking 6 hours, it now took 1 hour. The only danger had been to the person removing the fire crystals from the water tank, but this had been solved by only allowing the salamanders to complete this dangerous task. They were immune to the heat of the crystals and steam.

"Rosa, how are the Railway Defence Force shaping up?" Nirvana asked. Then she saw the shocked looks on Will and

Rosa's faces. "What? Oh, well there is no need to keep the secret of your death anymore, Rosa. Owen has served his purpose and we no longer need to protect him."

Will couldn't help but smile. He should have realised that Nirvana would have known that Zaran was a disguise that was no longer needed. She was always one step ahead of the rest of them!

Sometime later, Will and Rosa stood arm in arm, waiting for the inevitable. They had been dismissed from the council chambers and told to get some rest. There would be little down time from now on and it was important that they were at their best. But sleep was impossible, and they both knew that. So, they stood at the top of a small rise on the east side of the city, not far from the sanctuary they had visited when Will had first arrived. From there they could see the lights of the oncoming army's cooking fires. They stretched as far as the eye could see and Will didn't mind admitting that the sight terrified him. The sheer number of troops that Starin had at his disposal was mind-blowing. He couldn't understand what they were waiting for either.

"Why don't they just attack? What are they waiting for?"

"Daylight, probably. Fighting in the dark is hard. Fighting in daylight is tough enough, but at night, you can't see whether folk are friend or foe. Their numbers mean that they don't have to take that risk."

Shortly afterwards, Will and Rosa returned to her cabin and ate a meal. Neither was hungry but starving themselves wouldn't help. They sat and chatted for a while and then decided that they preferred being on the hill, watching over the city so they returned to their earlier spot and continued to watch the fires of the humans grow until there seemed to be no space left on the land outside the shield.

The pair sat, quietly watching when Rosa muttered something under her breath. She pointed into the darkness and asked Will if he saw anything strange. But Will didn't have the eyesight of a kitsune. All he could see was darkness.

"They are moving something, actually several things. They are long and cylindrical and on cart wheels. I can't make out the details but whatever these things are they are moving them to the front lines. They must be some kind of weapon."

"Wait, cylindrical? Are they narrower at the front than at the back?"

"It's difficult to tell for sure, but yes. I think they are. Do you know what they are?"

"If I had to guess, and this is a guess, Rosa, I would say they are cannons." Seeing her confused look, he went on. "They shoot a heavy ball of metal long distances, like the bullet from their rifles, but much bigger and they can do a lot more damage. It makes sense. If there have been other ships that have come from my world to this one, they almost certainly had some kind of weapons on them and cannons were often used on ships in historical times. This is bad, Rosa. The damage they can do is massive. A lot of folk are going to be killed if they are using cannons."

"Oh Will. Folk were always going to die. It is the price we are willing to pay for our freedom. What worries me more is that, if they are moving these cannons into place now, they are closer to attacking the walls than we thought. We need to get the trains out. Now! I must find Mother and tell her all you have told me. Come on."

Together they ran down the hill, to the council chambers

where, as expected, Nirvana was still making plans for the upcoming battle.

"Mother. We have news." Rosa called as they walked in the door.

Nirvana was about to give a short response to her daughter, which involved a stern reproach for disturbing her, but then she saw the look on Rosa's face and stopped herself. Nirvana was exhausted and the battle hadn't even started yet. Ah well. She would rest later.

Rosa briefed Nirvana on what they had seen, or rather, what they thought they had seen and they both agreed that it was time for the trains to get out of the city. It may already be too late, but they had to try. How Starin had managed to find them and get his army there so quickly was a mystery for another time.

It was the hour before dawn and preparations were well and truly underway when the first BOOM was heard. Starin's army hadn't waited until first light as the Council had expected they would. As soon as the cannons were in place, they were being fired. After the first shot, and the shock at the loudness of it, the noise became incessant. Crash after crash went into the protective barrier which had surrounded the City of Hope for so long. Each cannon ball was made from the same anti-magik metal that the human's armour was made from and each hit on the wall took its toll. It was still over an hour before the first cracks started showing though. By that time, Will was in Sherpa, working furiously alongside So'Ren and the other members of the Railway Defence Force. They knew the stakes couldn't be any higher. Steele and Ebunnie were amongst those getting folk onboard the carriages, making sure they were as safe as they could be. So'Ren was going to take Number 4, whilst Will and Rosa would drive his beloved Darjeeling through the barrier and take their precious cargo to the dwarven mines on the Plains of Aramanth and then onto the city of Anderbad. Then Will and Rosa would return to the battle for the City of Hope. That was the plan, anyway. As every commander knows though, a battle plan is only good until the battle starts.

After hours of bombardment, the shield around the City fell and the human army, led by Starin himself, poured in through the gap. Until that point there had been no way of getting the trains out of the city. The constant cannon strikes had meant that it would be suicide to venture out of the shield's protection. But now, their hand had been forced and Will threw open Sherpa's regulator and sped along the track, mowing down huge swathes of troops, under the rams that had been hastily installed onto Sherpa and Number 4, as he went. So'Ren followed his lead and the two engines ploughed through, followed by the soldiers of the Defence Force. Rosa was at the head of her troops as they fought their way through the enemy lines. The ground to the sides of the engines was slippery with the blood of both ally and enemy. Will could not believe the noise of the battle; the booming of the cannons, which were still firing into the City, the screams of the dead and dying, the clang of metal on metal and magikal explosions all around. It was like hell on earth and all Will could think about was that those he loved were down there, fighting for what they believed in, whilst he was safely tucked up in the cab of his engine. His friends were fighting for their homes, for their families and for their very way of life and the right to live without fear. But, as he cut his way through the enemy troops, he could see what a hopeless task this was. The amount of troops Starin had mustered was beyond anything they could have imagined or planned for and Will had the realisation that this was one of those occasions when the plan had to change.

"Rosa, we have to change the plan."

"I know. We need to get all folk out of the city. We cannot hold it."

The engines were all still pulling forward, and each had multiple crew on the footplate. Will suddenly had an idea.

"Keep going" he shouted at whoever was listening and then climbed out of the back of the cab and ran across the top of the carriages towards So'Ren in Number 4. So'Ren couldn't believe what Will was doing, but he knew he had to get as close to Sherpa as he could as Will was going to jump between the two trains.

"Are you crazy? What are you doing, you lunatic?" he screamed. It was if everything went into slow motion. He watched Will take a step backwards, then So'Ren inhaled sharply as his friend started to run forwards, images of Will falling onto the tracks and killing himself kept flashing in his vision. Will leapt through the air and landed on the ram at the front of his engine, but he stumbled as he landed and started to fall over the edge of the ram, towards the tracks below. At the last second, So'Ren saw Will grab the headlamp fitting and right himself. So'Ren exhaled sharply and gasped for his next breath, Then he watched Will scrambled up to the cab, grinning as he went.

"I have ALWAYS wanted to do that!" he laughed. "So'Ren, the plan is changing! Get these trains to the mines, I am going back for the Garratt. We are going to have to abandon the city for now and I need to get as many out as I can."

So'Ren stared Will in the eyes for what seemed like an hour. Then turned to his staff and asked for volunteers. He needed 2. They had to be fire breathers to charge up the fire crystals. There were no shortage of volunteers , and they quickly left via the back of the cab and over the carriages.

So'Ren skilfully slowed the engine just long enough for Will and his volunteers to leap off the back of the train and then he had the regulator open and was off after the Darjeeling engine.

Rosa had followed Will from the ground. She had gathered a small team around her, put her second in command in charge of the fleeing trains, and then made her way to the back of Number 4 to wait for Will. The fighting around the trains was fierce and they had all taken injuries, but they knew that Will and the Garratt were the only chance any of them had of getting out of there that day. So, they renewed their efforts and battled their way back to the city and into the engine sheds.

"We need an hour," Will shouted. He knew what he was asking of Rosa, but he also knew that hundreds of lives would be saved if he could get the engine up and running.

"You will have it, beloved," she replied.

Will got to work and Rosa sent a runner to her mother, telling her to gather as many as they could at the engine sheds. They were leaving. Rosa knew Nirvana would not like that plan, but she also knew that her mother was not a fool; she would see that the battle was lost. Rosa drew her katana once again. She would give Will that hour. She would give him more if it was within her.

When Will got to the sheds, the embers of the fires they had used earlier in the day were still glowing. The Garratt soon had a fire burning and the fire-breathers were heating as many fire crystals as they could. This was going to be the fastest steam up they had ever done! Meanwhile, every carriage that they could find was connected up behind the engine and everything in them was thrown out. They needed space to get as many out as they could.

Suddenly, the fighting was right outside the sheds. Screaming voices were everywhere and the clash of steel on steel echoed around the buildings. That could only mean that Nirvana had arrived. Folk started pouring into the sheds, many of them wounded and bleeding. The human attackers were following closely. Through the frantic activity needed to get the huge engine steaming, Will glimpsed Nirvana, right in the centre of the action. Her twin katanas flashing with every blow she made. She cut down everything in her path, but still more humans came.

Then, Starin himself appeared out of nowhere and the two leaders faced one another in combat. No-one had expected the human king to be present at the battle, let alone amongst the fighting. But there he was, standing in front of his nemesis. They had never met before, but they knew each other. Starin glared at the kitsune female with hatred in his eyes. Nirvana met his stare with her own, but hers was one of determination rather than hatred. They were well-matched. What Nirvana had in skill, Starin matched with strength. The battle was mesmerising and Will struggled to take his eyes off them and concentrate on his own tasks.

Then one of the fire-breathers, whose name Will didn't yet know, gave him the news he was desperate to hear. The engine was ready.

Will drew in a huge breath and bellowed at the top of his lungs

"Allied Magiks, to me!!!!"

Folk leapt onto the carriages and wagons connected to the Garratt and soon they were absolutely packed full of folk. They were still fighting off humans from the sides of the carriages when Will opened the regulator and started the huge engine rolling. It didn't get far before a huge crack sounded from underneath the engine.

"What the hell was that?" Will yelled, leaping down from the cab.

One of the brake pipes had burst. Quickly setting to work, Will soon had repairs underway. But Starin had also seen Will exiting the train. He broke off from his fight with Nirvana and leapt after Will. This human who had betrayed his kind would pay in blood. Will was so engrossed in his work that he didn't even see Starin approaching him. But Nirvana did. She sprinted round attackers and defenders alike, frantically trying to get to Will in time.

Starin's sword was raised ready to strike, when Nirvana leapt in front of him, bringing her katanas up to block the blow. But she was too late. Rather than blocking the blow with her katanas, she blocked it with her shoulder. Starin's sword cut deeply into Nirvana's body, and she fell.

Will finished his repairs and spun, ready to leap back into the cab. As he turned he saw Nirvana slipping to the floor, blood spraying from the horrific wound that ran across her body. Their eyes met and she mouthed the word "GO!" before her eyes closed for the last time.

Will obeyed. He grabbed Nirvana's broken body from

the floor and threw her into the cab. He leapt onto the footplate and opened the regulator once more. This time, the engine moved forward and started to gain speed. Rosa came flying onto the engine, sobbing, having seen her mother fall.

"Noooooooooo!" she screamed and threw her head back, howling. Then she leapt back off the engine and sought out Starin. She attacked in an absolute frenzy. He had never faced a kitsune in a rage before and he was already exhausted from the battle with Nirvana. Rosa scored many hits on him, but she too was injured from her defence of Will and the engines. As the Garratt passed where she was fighting with Starin, Will leant out and grabbed her, pulling her into the engine. He locked eyes with Starin

"You will pay for the hurt you have caused today. This I swear!"

And with that, the huge engine sped out of the city and away from the battle.

17

RECOVERY

The Garratt headed for Anderbad, the second City of the Allied Magiks. It was the only other large settlement that the Allied Magiks had and, whilst not as big as the City of Hope, it was still well equipped and the best place for planning the retaking of the City of Hope.

Just as the engine crossed the Etterdown Bridge, not far from the fallen City of Hope, a platoon of knights rode onto the bridge ahead of them and blocked their exit. Will was ready to plough right through them, but the Garratt had not been fitted with a ram and that could lead to the engine being derailed. Will couldn't risk the lives of all those onboard his engine and so brought the engine to a halt. Ahead of the train, something was fixed to the rails, which Will guessed were some sort of explosives. He was just about to turn to Rosa to tell her what was happening when he heard a sound that he had never expected to hear on Vitae.

Automatic gunfire!

As he was trying to figure out where the sound was coming from and how Starin managed to get hold of machine guns, the knights started falling like dominoes.

"What the Hell..."

From out of the undergrowth, several camouflaged figures emerged and approached the fallen knights. They checked them to ensure they were dead and then disarmed the explosives. When one of these newcomers gestured for the train to continue over the bridge, Will just nodded dumbly, blasted the whistle in acknowledgement, and did as he was told.

"What are you doing?" Rosa demanded from the floor of the cab, where she was sitting next to the covered form of her mother. It almost broke his heart to see the pain and anguish in her eyes, but he knew he had to carry on.

"I don't really know what is going on here, but we have just been rescued by... well... by soldiers from Earth."

Once the Garratt and its carriages had cleared the bridge, Will brought the train to a halt. The camouflaged man who had gestured the train across approached the cab and introduced himself.

"I am Sergeant Blackwood, from 45 Commando, Royal Marines. We are here to help and to return you home Mr Thorpe."

Before Blackwood could say another word, the sound of rapidly approaching horse beats could be heard from the other side of the bridge. They turned and saw Starin and some of his army heading for the other side of the bridge. Blackwood turned to his men and ordered the explosives on the bridge to be detonated and then they would depart on the engine to a place of relative safety.

Two Royal Marines charged back onto the bridge, reset the explosives and then one gave a signal to Blackwood before leaping off the bridge, and returning to the engine.

Blackwood told everyone to take cover and then detonated the explosives. The explosion was loud! Despite many of the folk knowing that it was coming, the noise made everyone on the train jump. Children and adults alike cried out in fear as the carriages rocked on their axles. When they looked back they saw that the bridge was completely destroyed and many of the human army had fallen to their deaths or were gored by flying splinters of the wooden bridge. Once the debris had settled, Will, Rosa and Blackwood looked back to the other side of the former Etterdown bridge. Starin was still there, glaring at them and Will found himself wondering at the luck of the man. How he had escaped the destruction of the bridge, Will would never know. But, for now, the Allied Magiks were safe, so he climbed back into the Garratt's cab and set off once more, this time with a few extra passengers, and a bit more hope.

The arrival of the Garrattt at Anderbad was a solemn affair. It had taken them many hours to get to the city, all the while carrying the beloved leader of the Folk of Vitae. Will could feel Rosa's pain, through the heart bond they shared. It was almost enough to break him, but he knew there was no-one else who could drive this engine. He had to get Rosa to Anderbad and allow her to grieve in peace for a while.

As they travelled, Blackwood filled Will on what he was doing there.

"The truck that exploded back in Scotland had been carrying a prototype wormhole generator." Seeing Will's confused look, he explained "It's classified, but I can tell you that it allows travel from one realm to another and we have been using it to try and get to the bottom of some of the strange occurrences at home. Disappearing ships and planes. That sort of thing. There has been an increase recently so we need to find out what was going on. When my boss heard of your disappearance, and that of the trains..."

"Engines" Rosa whispered from her place on the floor. Will couldn't help but smile a little at that.

"... what? Oh right, engines, sorry. I was ordered to come and find you and bring you home."

As Blackwood talked about bringing Will "home" Will felt a stabbing pain in his chest. He gasped and almost doubled over.

"What's wrong?" Blackwood asked "Medic!"

"Nothing. It's fine. I am not hurt." Will knew that the pain wasn't his. It was Rosa's. The thought of losing her love, having so recently lost her mother was almost too much for her to bear.

"I am not going anywhere, Blackwood. Vitae is my home now and I am not leaving."

Will felt an instant lifting of the pain in his chest.

"You don't understand what is happening here," Will told the Sergeant. For the rest of the journey, Will filled Blackwood in on everything that had happened since his arrival. Blackwood was very interested to hear about the technology that was being used on Vitae, especially when Will explained about the War Engine and Alco being engines from Earth.

"That might explain a few things," Blackwood said thoughtfully. "This is all above my pay grade but, I know there had been some discussion about technology, and people, going missing. Something to do with the Bermuda Triangle, but I don't really know anything else. As I say, I am just a lowly Sergeant, but I will let my Commanding Officer know about it when we next check in. She will be very interested in what has been happening here. In the meantime, we will help as much as we can."

"Good. Because I mean to make Starin pay dearly for this." Will gestured to the floor; to his beloved Rosa and to the body of the woman who had been like a mother to him since his arrival in Vitae.

Several hours later, they arrived in Anderbad. Word of the death of Nirvana quickly spread and the mood was very sombre. Rosa had barely spoken a word since scrambling into the cab with the ruined body of her mother. The shock of losing Nirvana was weighing her down and she barely acknowledged the presence of anyone else. Will had some experience of this grief. He had lost both of his parents 3 years earlier when they had been in a horrific car crash, and he had barely come up for air for 6 months. It had only been when he heard about the Darjeeling shell that was just waiting to be restored, that he had found something to live for again. He had thrown himself into that work and back into his apprenticeship at the Ginger Line and it had saved him. So, he knew that Rosa needed a purpose. She needed time to grieve but she didn't have that luxury right now. They were at war and the Folk of Vitae needed a leader. Rosa was that leader, she just needed to realise it.

On arrival at the train yards in Anderbad, the local council members had made the arrangements and Nirvana's body was taken to be prepared for the ceremony of departure. The loss of the City of Hope, and its Garden of Remembrance, was felt keenly that day. Will vowed that he would make sure that Nirvana was honoured in her rightful place and that he would retake the City of Hope from Starin. Rosa, Nirvana and all the folk who had lost loved ones, deserved nothing less.

Will guided Rosa to the council chambers at the centre of Anderbad. He talked to her the whole way and, slowly, she started to come back to awareness of their situation. It was when Will had asked if she wanted to surrender to Starin that she had whirled on him, with her knives out and her eyes flashing. Her tails had swished and bristled, and her ears were pressed flat to her head.

"I will never surrender to that monster!"

"Right then. Your people need a leader, and you are the one they want. You don't have the time to grieve now. That will come later, when we retake the City of Hope and can remember Nirvana in her rightful resting place. Right now, we need to find homes for these folk and come up with a plan of attack. Are you ready?"

Rosa stared at Will with her flashing eyes and her knives still raised. Then she visibly wilted, and a single tear rolled down her ashen face.

"How will I do this without my mother at my side?" she whispered.

"You will prevail. You are the strongest women I have ever met. Even stronger than your mother. You stood up to her when no-one else would. You can do this."

General Ember approached them and cleared his throat.

"Rosa, I need you! I am sorry for your loss, but your folk are scared and only you can reassure them."

Rosa squared her shoulders, re-sheathed her blades and strode after Ember. In that moment she became the new leader of the Folk of Vitae, whether voted for or not, she would not allow her folk to be lost at a time like this. Elections could come later.

During the next days, Sgt. Blackwood's team, with permission from Rosa, maintained a watch on the perimeter of Anderbad. They knew that Starin's army would follow them to the new home of the Allied Magiks and a watchful eye and early warning were their best defence at that time. The Royal Marines were also given permission to start training the Allied Magiks in modern combat techniques. The best way to defeat the invaders was to fight them in an unfamiliar way; make themselves unpredictable.

A week after their arrival in Anderbad, So'Ren and the engines that had been sent to the plains of Aramanth steamed into the station. Word had been sent to them of the death of Nirvana and their mood was low when they pulled in. But, they brought some good news with them.

"Look. Up there," So'Ren instructed Will and Rosa.

At first, they could see nothing at all as the sun was shining brightly, but then, like lightning bolts streaking from the cloudless sky, three dragons came into view. Their gleaming scales caught the sunlight as they came, giving them a strange glow. The iridescent gleaming was mesmerising, and Will couldn't take his eyes of the huge figures.

Obsidian was the first to land. Will couldn't help but sneak a look at Blackwood. Until now, the stoic sergeant had been unflappable, but surely seeing a dragon for the first time would shake him? Will was a little disappointed, therefore, to only see a slight quirk in Blackwood's eyebrows. Nothing seemed to phase the man.

Rosa stepped forward to address the huge, black beast.

"Beloved Obsidian. I am Rosa, daughter of Nirvana, who has passed from this life, into the next."

Obsidian and the two dragons with him, through back their huge heads and howled. Fire leapt from their jaws and the heat could be felt by all the folk present. After a long moment, Obsidian blinked, allowing tears to escape from his huge black eyes.

"Ahhh, Darling Rosa. I see you and love you. My sadness at the loss of blessed Nirvana is great and I will avenge her death as best I can. Will you have my brethren and I? Will you allow us to help you rid this world of the disease that is Starin?"

"Beloved Obsidian. I thank you for seeing me. Never could I refuse you. Your aid in our time of need is most gratefully accepted."

After many more flowery speeches, and much time, Obsidian and his companions were introduced to Blackwood and plans for the retaking of the City of Hope were drawn up. The dragons loved the idea of "Air Raids"on Starin's Army. They would not expect that. Never before had the dragons taken such an active role in a battle, but their love of Nirvana had been fierce and their anger at her loss was equally so.

During the planning and training, So'Ren was, surprisingly, absent. One rainy morning, when Rosa was attending a council meeting, Will went to find his friend. He went over to the engine sheds and found So'Ren surrounded by drawings and designs. They were spread all over the workshop and were incredibly detailed.

"What are these, So'Ren?"

So'Ren was concentrating so closely on his work that he

hadn't noticed Will Come into the sheds.

"What? Oh, you made me jump, Will. When did you come in?

"I have only just got here. What are you designing? Are these cannons? And these, steam engines?" Will looked at his friend with amazement.

"Well, yes, I... I didn't want to sssay anything as I may not be able to get it to work, but I think..."

At that moment, Blackwood strode into the sheds. He had just returned from his patrol and was heading for a hot meal and his bed for a few hours. But, when he saw the designs in Will's hands, curiosity got the better of him.

"Ha. A steam tank. That's a great idea. When can you have it ready by?"

So'Ren's skin turned an even deeper green, which was his version of blushing. He always blushed when his work was praised, and it drove Will mad that his friend had so little confidence in himself. So'Ren was an engineering genius, and everyone knew it. Everyone except So'Ren that was.

"Well, I don't know about that. I jussst thought that if we built an engine that protected the driver and allowed a weapon to be fired at the sssame time, we might have an advantage over Ssstarin. He would not expect it. I didn't know if I could make it work, but I think I can."

Blackwood and So'Ren spent several hours in the sheds discussing ways to improve the design of the steam tank. For the next days any folk, or Royal Marine, who had knowledge that would help, were called to the sheds to provide assistance. It wasn't long before the first steam tank was being built. But there was a problem. The dwarves were struggling to provide enough coal to keep the steam engines running. Over the past week, none of the engines had been run, but that was due to Will, So'Ren and the RDF having other responsibilities: getting folk from the City of Hope settled and having any injuries treated. But that wouldn't be the case for much longer and it was vital that the engines were kept in a state of readiness, should Starin's army attack. Losing the bridge had slowed the human army down as that route was the only one that would take the amount of traffic that the army created. However, the time was coming when the Allied Magiks would need all their resources at the ready if they were going to stand a chance at defeating Starin. This meant that So'Ren had had to be creative when it came to powering the steam tanks, or "Armoured Mobile Cannon Vehicle" as he had originally named it.

So'Ren had found a way to harness the power of fire crystals to heat the boilers. The dull, orange crystals were much more plentiful than coal and were used widely by folk, as a heat source. So'Ren had already been thinking of the best ways to use the more powerful infernoss crystals to power Will's engines and so, when the tanks were needed, had a basic idea of what he needed to achieve. He had quickly built a test engine to see whether his plans would work and all involved were stunned at how efficiently the little engine heated the boiler, and at how long that heat remained constant.

"So'Ren, you are a genius. I cannot believe how well this works. Can you do the same to Sherpa? I don't want to take you away from the steam tanks, but, if you have the time, that will make a big difference."

"I can, but I am going to use infernosss crystals for the engines. They are much bigger and need more power. I already have the plansss here and will ssstart work sssoon. I am going to do both Sherpa and the Garratt asss they are the most usseful to us. I may be able to upgrade the Alco asswell but it will depend on how much time we have. For now, leave Sherpa cold and I will get her done firssst."

"You are a legend!" Will replied. He felt like a child at Christmas. This upgrade would change everything. It would make the engines much faster to get ready and much more efficient. Will knew the dwarves would be very grateful for not having to mine so much coal.

Whilst Will was excited about the upgrades to Sherpa, he was also struggling with his guilt over Nivana's death. He blamed himself for her death. If he had maintained the engines better, the brake pipe wouldn't have burst, and he wouldn't have needed saving. If he had been a better engineman, Nirvana would still be alive, and Rosa wouldn't be suffering so much.

Will threw himself into combat training to try and alleviate some of this guilt. If he was stronger and fitter and faster, he would be better. Of course, this wasn't true and Will's friends told him as much, but grief and guilt were all he could feel at that time. Rosa could feel Will's guilt and shame through the heart bond, but it was all she could do to deal with her own pain, and that of her people. She could only reassure him that he had nothing to feel guilty about and that Nirvana's death was not laid at his door, but at Starins.

Meanwhile, in Starin's army, things were going from bad to worse. The king was losing his grip on reality and growing madder by the day. He had executed many of his officers after the battle of the City of Hope. The battle had been a success, but Starin had wanted every single Allied Magik slaughtered, and many had escaped. Added to that was the loss of his Alco and the trains that the human, who was with the Allied Magiks, had brought to Vitae. Starin's anger was almost uncontrollable, and his remaining generals were starting to worry. Now that Steele had left his father's army, they would need an heir, someone to put on the throne, someone they could control easily enough. Just as the generals were starting to think that things couldn't get worse, rocks and fire started falling on them from the sky!

18
THE FUTURE OF WARFARE

All was quiet in Anderbad. There had been no sightings of Starin's Army, mainly due to the massive success of the bombing campaign that the Allied Magiks had been running against them. No-one could have predicted how successful the dragons would be. Not only were they successful, but they were enjoying the whole process of destroying the army's ability to manoeuvre.

Initially the dragons had just tried to do as much damage as possible, whether that be to man or machine. But, after a few days they realised that they didn't actually want to kill the humans. Having met Will and Owen Trelisker, who was quickly becoming a firm favourite in Anderbad, they realised that humans weren't all bad. They were just being led by corrupt people. So, from that moment on, they had aimed at the army's infrastructure, their war machines. The dragons were actually a fairly peaceful race, but their sheer size and power made them appear fearsome. However, killing any living thing had bothered them greatly. Once they had realised that this wasn't necessary, they had started to thoroughly enjoy their bombing runs and took great pride in the pinpoint accuracy that they could achieve.

The phenomenal success of the dragons had meant that the Allied Magiks had had the time they needed to build their own war machines. The steam powered armoured cannon vehicles were being built and the first one was conducting trials. According to Sergeant Blackwood, they were loosely based on the British Mark 4 tank which was used in World War 1 and had a pair of steam funnels mounted side by side and a pair of 6lb cannons, which they had initially liberated from Starin's Alco. However, once So'Ren and his team of engineers had got hold of them, many improvements had been made. Now, they were much lighter and able to throw a projectile a lot further. They were also able to launch magik projectiles much further than any of the folk could, which was a huge improvement to their fighting capabilities. They still had to be drawn back into the tank to be reloaded and those operating the cannons complained about the awful conditions inside the tanks, but all in all, these machines were a huge upgrade on the Allied Magik's weaponry and hope was rising that the new year approaching would be one filled with peace, rather than one filled with fear.

The tanks quickly became known as Steel Minotaurs and the Council were debating where they should first be deployed against Starin's Army. There was really only one answer, and that was the retaking of the City of Hope. Folk wanted to go home, despite being made very welcome in Anderbad. The dragons had been reporting on the situation in the City of Hope, so the council knew that since their evacuation, the city had been turned into a fortress and, worse than that, the War Engine was there and ready to be put to use. Despite this, it was agreed that this was the best place to start, and Rosa would lead their troops into battle, aided by the Royal Marines. The fight would not be easy, but that didn't mean the plan was a complicated one. Surround the city and lay siege to it. Their extended range weapons gave them an advantage that the humans wouldn't be expecting and with the support of the dragons thrown in for good measure, the Allied Magiks were in a good position to retake their beloved city.

A date had been set for the Battle for the City and a few days before, Prince Steele had come to see Rosa and Will.

Steele had been trying to make himself useful, as he had in the city, but he was still unpopular amongst the folk of Vitae. They just couldn't get over the fact that he was Starin's son. But Will and Rosa had spent a little time with him and Ebunnie and, whilst they were still cautious about what they discussed with him, they actually quite liked him. He was a calm, sensible young man, who was thoughtful and considerate. Despite the treatment he had received at the hands of some of the folk, he was slow to anger and happy to aid when needed. Steele had been training with the RDF and latterly, with the tanks, becoming a proficient driver and an excellent shot with a cannon. But it was not intended to put him into battle in the steel minotaurs and this was what he wanted to talk to Rosa about.

"I know you don't fully trust me, and I understand that.."

"I don't understand that," the fiery Ebunnie chipped in, receiving a look from Steele that suggested they had had this conversation many times before. The look didn't stop Ebunnie from stamping her little foot several times and flicking her ears. Steele couldn't help but smile. Ebunnie trying to look cross was probably when she looked at her cutest.

"... but I want to be part of the battle. I am a good driver and an even better shot. I can make small repairs and am not afraid to go up against my father's army."

"This isn't about trusting you, Steele. This is about you being accepted by a tank's crew. You know how important it is for the crew to all work in harmony with each other. Don't worry. I am not leaving you out of the battle. I have something else in mind for you and young Owen, if he is willing." Steele nodded as Will explained what he had in mind.

Plans for the siege went well and everything was in place for the Allied Magiks to depart from Anderbad when a dragon flew into the city and roared for Rosa. Having seen that the dragon, whose name was Carnelian, was approaching, Rosa was already on her way to the meeting place.

"I am here, beloved Carnelian. What has you so anxious?"

"The human, Starin, has left the city and he has taken the abomination with him. Now is the time for you take your city back. Hurry, dear one, hurry!"

Rosa didn't pause for a moment. She was giving orders and getting folk moving within seconds. The abomination that Carnelian referred to was the War Engine. The biggest problem with their plans had been how to neutralise the effects of its noxious red gas and it was to this that Will had been referring when he had told Steele that he had a mission in mind for them. However, if the engine wasn't in the City of Hope, they had a much greater chance of victory, to say nothing about losing less magik-users to the gas and the anti magik armour. They knew that Starin and the engine leaving the city could have been a trap, but it was a chance thcy had to take in order to save as many folk as they could.

Preparations were already complete and all it would take to depart was to get the engines steamed up and folk in the right place. Now that Sherpa had an infernoss crystal in place of its firebox, starting it up took less than an hour. In fact, Sherpa was ready to go before most of the folk were. The Alco and No. 4 took a little longer as they were still relying on the fire-breathers to heat their boilers, but within 3 hours, the Allied Magiks were setting off to retake the City of Hope.

Anderbad was a beautiful city and the folk living there had given as much as they could to make their City of Hope guests comfortable but cramming a whole city worth of folk into the already busy Anderbad had caused some frayed tempers. Fights and scuffles had broken out and old disputes, some of which had led to the founding of the second city many years ago, were raised again. It had not been the easiest of times for the folk of Vitae, but now they were all working together to bring the City of Hope back into their hands once more.

Early the next morning, the troops and machinery of the Allied Magiks were back at the bridge which Blackwood had blown up in order to protect them from Starin's army. Since the plans had been drawn up to retake the City of Hope, work had started on rebuilding the bridge. Everyone had known that the bridge was vital to their plans and so, a team of engineers had been working on a way to get the engines and troops safely across without making it accessible to Starin's army. Starin had been trying to do the same thing from the other side and had made some progress towards stabilising the destroyed structure. They had sunk a pillar into the canyon which the bridge spanned and the Vitae engineers had been able to factor this pillar into their calculations. The Royal Marines had suggested using something along the lines of a pontoon bridge which could be slipped into place and removed fairly easily, but this one would not float on water. This idea had been approved and the sky pontoon had been developed. It was made from magikally enhanced steel and could easily take the massive weight of the army's machinery but was light enough to be manoeuvred into place with help of the dragons. Once the army had passed over the bridge, a small contingent of defenders would remain, just in case the bridge needed to be raised to prevent Starin's troops from crossing it and storming the passes which led to Anderbad.

The tanks had been partially dismantled before leaving Anderbad and were being carried to the battlefield, either by dragon or in wagons on the back of the engines. Once at the City of Hope, engineers quickly put the tanks back together and prepared them for the attack on the City. Four had been built and it was hoped that more could be created in the future, if they were needed, but finding the raw materials in sufficient quantity was going to be a challenge. So'Ren had plans in mind to remedy the shortage, but he hadn't really had the time to do more than plan at that point.

Now, with the Allied Magiks in place, the tanks reassembled and the Royal Marines ready to use their arsenal of weapons against the occupying army, the attack could start. The dragons were the first wave. With the folk still out of sight, a flight of dragons headed up and over the walls of the city, dropping huge boulders to distract the humans from the approach of the tanks. It worked well. The humans had experienced the attacks of the dragons for several weeks now and they knew how devastatingly accurate the beasts were. They took cover as best they could and so, didn't notice the tanks until they were in firing range. The dragons dropped one last load onto the city and then withdrew from the field. Just as the humans started poking their heads up over the newly-created palisade, the tanks fired. The sound was breathtaking.

BOOM! They fired. BOOM BOOM. Again and again, magical, and non-magikal, projectiles flew over the walls and into the legions of troops standing behind them. Smoke floated over the cleared ground around the walls and the smell of gunpowder was strong in the air. The humans didn't know what had hit them. For far too long they had been the stronger army and they were still surprised whenever the Allied Magiks attacked so fiercely. They had not learnt anything from their losses at Sea Town and were still using the same old tactics, which were getting them nowhere in this siege. The very idea of being held under siege by the Allied Magiks was laughable. The Allied Magiks just didn't fight like that.

Well, they did now!

Blackwood and his team were poised at the gates and ready to enter the city. Will had his train mounted cannons aimed at the main city gates and as soon as they smashed through, Blackwood would force entry. Rosa gave the signal and the cannons fired. Their aim was true, and the gates splintered at the first salvo. The second took them clean off their hinges. Once the gates were gone, it was only a matter of time before the city was back in the hands of the Allied Magiks. The humans just couldn't stand up to the might of the superior weaponry of the Royal Marines and the sheer power of the tanks.

This didn't mean that the human army didn't put up a good fight. They did. Blood and broken bodies covered the ground within the walls of the city. In the end though, humans laid down their weapons in droves with many trying to flee into the night. Most were caught and held by the Allied Magik army. Once again, the humans were put to work, clearing the dead and removing the gore from the streets. They were made to carry the wounded of both sides to the makeshift infirmaries which were quickly set up inside the city. The humans were amazed that their enemies were treating their injuries without malice. It was this act alone that started to turn the tide of opinion amongst the humans as they knew that, if the tables had been turned, they would not have been permitted to help the wounded Allied Magiks. They would have been ordered to put them to death.

That night, after efforts had started to shore up the City's defences, and Will had finished helping at the infirmary which was treating the human soldiers, Rosa and Will took a walk back to her cabin to see if it was still standing. They had known that there was a chance that the city would have been flattened, by the dragon's bombardment and by the malevolence of the human generals, and whilst the damage was extensive, Rosa's cabin was mostly unscathed with just a couple of broken window panels. Her garden would take some time to put right. The flowers had been trampled and some of the beautiful, scented shrubs had been pulled out and cast aside. Branches were broken from some of the smaller trees and someone had obviously started a cook fire on the small lawn. But it could have been much, much worse. As they were standing amongst the trampled flowers, Rosa gasped and ran over to a tree. There, hung from a branch, was one of Nirvana's scarves. She had been wearing it the last time they had gathered in the garden and must have dropped it. Rosa wrapped the scarf in her hands and was suddenly kneeling on the floor racked by sobs. She had not had time to fully process the loss of her mother and the scarf had brought it all back to the surface. Will ran to her side and pulled her into his lap. He held her close, stroking her back and letting her cry. They stayed like that for a long time. Will cried with Rosa for some time but finally, exhausted, they pulled apart and sat looking at each other.

"I missed you," she whispered.

Since their arrival in Anderbad, both had been consumed by the roles they had had to take on; she as the leader of the Folk of Vitae and he as the chief engineer in the RDF. Neither had had the luxury of spending time with a loved one, barely even seeing each other for meals. Will was also ashamed to admit that he had feared facing Rosa. He was the person who had got her mother killed and he was terrified of seeing hatred towards him in her eyes.

"I am sorry. I didn't think you would want to see me."

"What? Why? I don't understand."

"Nirvana. She died saving me. It was my fault. If I had maintained the engines better, the brake pipe wouldn't have burst, and Nirvana wouldn't have had to save me. I am so sorry, Rosa. I will understand if you don't want to see me again."

"Will, you idiot. My mother's death is on the hands of Starin, not you. You saved her people and for that, you will always be a hero to the folk. I love you and she did too. So, I don't want to hear another word about her death being down to you. Do you hear me?" Rosa's tail was spread out in a fan behind her, and her ears were flattened to her head. She was angry with him, but then she relaxed and pulled him into her arms. She couldn't stay angry for long!

"I tell you this, beloved. We will avenge my mother's death and Starin will pay dearly for taking her from us. And for making me leader of the community, which is not a job that allows for much sitting around. So come on, we have work to do."

19
REACTIONS

The retaking of the City of Hope sent shock waves through every community, folk and humans alike. Never before had such an event occurred and, whilst there was still the War Engine and the king to deal with, the victory over the much larger, and seemingly better equipped army was staggering. Rebel groups started appearing throughout the realm and many were made up of humans dissatisfied with Starin's rule. Starin's army was struggling to keep control, having already lost many of their numbers in the battle for the City of Hope and his rule was starting to crumble.

The loss of the city had sent Starin into a tailspin, growing madder by the day. He could not believe that his army was losing to the magik scum. Where had they got the mechanised vehicles from, and those rapid-firing weapons. His enemy was developing technology that was better than his own and he couldn't understand how. When Starin had started to bring ships and aircraft through the portals, he had thought that he would win the war on magik in no time. But it had taken a lot longer than he had anticipated, to reverse engineer the technology and find a way to implement it and in that time his enemy had found a way to neutralise his advantage. The hatred Starin felt for the Allied Magiks' pet human was white hot. He knew he had to destroy the human and punish the scum who harboured him. Killing Nirvana was a sweet victory, but even that hadn't stopped them from defeating his army and re-taking their city. And to top all of this, his cursed son had joined the magik scum and was helping them to defeat him. His own son! Who he had cared for and taught how to rule. Steele had betrayed him, and he would pay for that with his life and that of the pooka that had left with him. Starin knew he would have to deploy his entire arsenal of secret weaponry, in order to defeat the rebellion and make the scum pay for trying to humiliate him.

Starin sent orders for every bit of technology he had to be prepared for use against the enemy army. As the terrified messenger ran from the room to deliver the message to Havesh, he could hear the King screeching with maniacal laughter. He exchanged a frightened look with the guards standing outside the king's door, who looked as concerned as he was. They could see that there wasn't much time before Starin completely lost control and knew that was going to be very bad for them.

When Havesh got the message that the King wanted all his secret weapons made ready for the attack on the Allied Magiks, he was worried. Yes, they had recovered many, many things from the other world, but none of them were ready to use. They had found a few vehicles with a strange hard black substance on the wheels, but they had only just found a fuel source for them and that was entirely by accident. After trying everything he could think of, Havesh had, in a drunken stupor, poured some of his liquor into the fuel recess. To his shock, when he turned the machine on, it coughed, spluttered, threw out plumes of foul-smelling black smoke and then had started to roar.

On the back of these strange vehicles was some kind of weapon, and in boxes next to these weapons were what appeared to be projectiles which were attached to some kind of net-like substance.

Havesh hadn't spent much time with these weapons before. Starin had insisted that the steam engines were going to be the ultimate attack vehicle and so there had been little time left over to satisfy his curiosity over how they worked. However, seeing the humans use their new technology had allowed Havesh to understand more about the ones they had hidden away in the storage area. The rapid firing weapons that the Allied Magik army had been using looked very similar to those on the back of the black wheels. After spending some time tinkering with the mechanisms, Havesh discovered how the projectiles were loaded into the weapon, then he had found the trigger and fired. The sound had been stunning within the enclosed cavern Havesh had been working in. It had taken a few minutes for him to recover, but once he had, and he looked at the rock face that the projectiles had hit, he knew he had made a huge discovery. These weapons would put them back in control of the situation. Havesh hummed gently to himself as he sent a messenger to the king and then started writing a list of the supplies he would need to get these machines ready for combat. Now that he had figured out the projectile weapons, and the black wheels, Havesh thought he knew how some of the other items worked as well. Excitement bubbled up in his evil chest and he couldn't wait to see the weapons used against his people.

20
BITING BACK

The Allied Magiks were on a roll! They were capturing strategic targets daily and more than that, humans living in the villages and towns outside of their capital city were joining the ranks of the Folk every day. This had led to a certain amount of friction amongst some of the Folk, but with the sheer numbers of humans now living amongst them, they were getting used to it.

In order to reduce the tensions within the army of the Folk of Vitae, Prince Steele had taken command of the humans who were willing to fight against the King. Owen Trelisker had been promoted to his second in command and the two of them quickly created an effective division of soldiers. Sgt Blackwood had helped to train them in all forms of combat, and they had developed a truly effective fighting force of which Steele was rightly proud. Owen was an excellent second in command, using his natural charm to ease tensions and when that didn't work, he wasn't afraid to kick butt! A firm friendship developed between Steele and Owen and Will was always pleased to see the two laughing together and supporting each other.

One of the humans who had come over to the Allied Magik banner was a man named Francis and he was a former member of the kings Special Operations Branch. These were the people who were the first to try out the new weapons that Havesh developed. Francis had worked on the armour and weaponry of the War Engine but seeing the effect of the red gas had broken him. He had decided that it was time for him to retire and had left the castle on the pretence of visiting family for a few days as his mother, who had actually died many years earlier, was sick. Francis had headed for a remote village, intending never return to Starin's castle again. When he had joined the Allied Magiks, Francis had approached Prince Steele and told him what he knew of the king's weaponry, offering to upgrade the Allied Magiks' cannons to make them more efficient. Now, instead of having to be pulled back into the tanks to be loaded, the cannons could be "breech loaded" through the back, meaning that they could be reloaded much more quickly, and more efficiently, than before. Francis had also been developing a river boat which was powered by steam and knew that this would be of use in the future. He was planning on making a living by building the boats before he joined the Allied Magiks. But he re-drew the designs to add elemental machine cannons once he learnt how effective elemental magik was when fired out of the tanks cannons. Having built boats in the past, it only took Francis and his team a few weeks to build a very basic prototype of the river boat. Once done, there had been some pressure on Will to have a race with Sherpa, but he had refused.

"Sherpa was built for climbing hills, not for speed. If I try and push her to go too fast, I could damage her and, at the moment, I can't replace anything that breaks," he insisted. His answer had gone down like a lead balloon, but he would not change his mind.

One morning Will was doing his routine maintenance on Sherpa when Rosa sent a message, summoning him to a council meeting. The note didn't give any details, but Will knew that Rosa wouldn't call him in unless it was something really important. When he arrived, Steele and So'Ren were already in their places and they both gave him a welcoming nod. Both shrugged their shoulders at his questioning look. They didn't know what was happening either. To add to the confusion, Blackwood was also present at the meeting. Then Rosa entered the chamber and the meeting started.

"Good morning. I will get straight to the point of this meeting. General Ember, Stormwind, Sgt Blackwood and I have been working on a plan to end this war. The plan is now complete, and we feel that we are ready to take Starin down."

Rosa paused as the council members started to whisper to each other in astonishment. Finally, Veneema, the female Naga, spoke up.

"Rosa, you know I support any attack on huma... Starin," Veneema, glanced at Steele and Blackwood. "He is a pox on this world, and he needs to be removed. But you made this plan without consulting the council members and that is not acceptable. We should be involved in all decisions," she continued. Veneema did not believe in hereditary titles and did not like the fact that Rosa had stepped into Nirvana's shoes without so much as a vote. There was no real doubt that Rosa would have been chosen by the Allied Magiks, had there been a vote, but Veneema still made sure that everyone knew she was unhappy about the situation.

"Really, Veneema? You feel that I should run every decision past you? Every decision? Including which way the sewage pipes should be laid and which buildings need new roofs this season? Every decision? Are you sure?"

Veneema grumbled and moaned a little but conceded the point. Rosa continued.

"I realise that these plans are slightly more important than some of the other decisions I need to make, but I wanted to keep the circle of those who knew the details small. As Will says, 'Loose lips sink ships' and this is one ship we don't want to sink."

Will couldn't help but notice Blackwood's slight smirk when Rosa used this saying. Will could feel himself blushing; that was hardly his saying! He grinned back at Blackwood and turned his attention back to Rosa.

"I apologise for keeping you all in the dark, but secrecy is essential as we have so many new folk in the city and we don't know that all of them are our friends."

"Forgive me Rosssa, but I thought we were many months away from being ready for this sscale of attack," So'Ren commented.

Rosa looked over to Sgt. Blackwood and gestured to him for a response.

"Following recent reconnaissance missions, conducted by myself and the men in my command, it has come to light that Starin's kingdom is on the brink of collapse. All it would take is one final massive assault and he will fall. I have spoken to my commander, Field Marshal Von Schrader, and she has given me approval to assist you in this assault, in order to achieve a successful outcome," Blackwood reported.

It took a second for the Council to digest the sergeant's report, but once they had, they all started talking at once. The excitement was palpable, and Will could almost feel the hope beginning to grow. Would they finally be able to live in peace, without the threat of being attacked at any moment? He looked over at Steele, who was grinning from ear to ear.

"You do realise that you will be fighting against the people you grew up with, don't you?" Will asked him. He knew it was a harsh statement, but Will wasn't sure that Steele appreciated the gravity of this situation.

"I do know that, but these are my people. I am their prince, and it is my duty to protect them. Cutting out the disease at the heart of the kingdom is what I am here to do. If I must fight, and kill, old friends to achieve that, then so be it!" he replied grimly.

Will nodded and then turned back to Rosa. She and Blackwood were about to lay out the plan before the council members.

Blackwood started "The plan is codenamed Operation Grand Slam and will be a night raid on Starin's castle. Every available resource will be committed to this attack. Nothing will be held in reserve. This is risky, but I feel it is justified. All four engines will be in play, so please ensure that you have all the supplies you need for that, Will. We are going to clad the engines in lightweight armour, especially your Sherpa. Without a cab, you would be very vulnerable in there."

The discussion took several hours and, at the end of it, Will felt confident that they had done everything they could to prepare for the battle. It worried him that everyone he knew was taking part in this battle and it was very possible that they would not return. Even Ebunnie would be there, as a nurse in the field hospital. She had thrived in the medica's charge. She was a force of nature and Will could see why Steele had fallen in love with her.

Over the next few days, Will and Rosa spent as much time as they could together, which wasn't much as they both had a huge workload, to ensure everything was ready for the attack. Will was worried about Rosa. He knew how she felt about him as he could feel it through the heart bond they shared. If he didn't make it back, so soon after losing Nirvana, Will wasn't sure that Rosa would recover. He tried to talk to her about his fears, but she just looked him in the eyes and told him that he had to come back, there was no other option. So, they sat in her garden; their favourite spot, and watched the sun set behind the mountains.

"Will, I have a gift for you. We, kitsune that is, don't usually give gifts but I know that your kind do, so I thought that I would give you this," Rosa blushed and stuttered. She was not used to being unsure of herself and gift giving was definitely not something she had done before. She shoved a leather-bound package at Will and then dropped it in his lap as if it would burn her. Then she snatched her hands back and sat on them, frowning as she did it.

Will couldn't help but laugh at Rosa's discomfort. She was probably the most capable person he had ever met and the simple act of giving a gift had her in such a kerfuffle! She blushed, wrapped and unwrapped her tail, flattened her ears and then laughed along with him.

Will unwrapped the package and gasped. Rosa had given him a beautiful, hand carved bow and a quiver full of arrows. He recognised the carving style as well. She had done the work herself, of that, he was sure.

"I don't know what to say. This is stunning. Thank you, Rosa." Will bent to kiss her and they stayed in the garden, in each other's arms, for the rest of the night.

The next morning, they left for the battle. The mood was sombre as all equipment was loaded and everyone boarded the trains and river steamers.

Will, Rosa and So'Ren were aboard the Darjeeling, and they led the convoy out of the City of Hope, ready for what they hoped would be the final battle in this war.

21
THE BATTLE BEGINS

Getting everyone into position outside the city of Stronghelm didn't happen overnight. In fact, it took several days, and this was time that Starin used well. Both sides had had time to build up their weaponry and Havesh had been exceptionally busy! Once he had sorted the black wheels out, he had discovered several crates marked with the word 'Vickers'. Inside were smaller versions of the black wheel's weapons along with the projectiles which they fired. These had been handed out for testing and now, many of the army companies were equipped with one of these Vickers. Havesh knew that they would be invaluable to Starin's forces, and he was excited to see their effects.

The Vickers weren't the only things Havesh had found though. There had been a crate which contained round shaped objects with a round pin in the top. The crate was marked with the word 'Grenade' and a warning that it contained explosives and that was enough to make Havesh very cautious for once. He soon realised the purpose of these grenades and ordered the testing of them as quickly as he could. He was almost gibbering with excitement at the amount of destruction the grenades could deploy.

Spies from the Allied Magiks had been able to get a good look at some of Starin's new weaponry, but they had not been able to get into the lab where Francis had told them that the weapons were tested and stored. This meant that there was a lot of uncertainty in the Allied Magik camp. Blackwood had been able to bring some advanced technology through the portal and so they were fairly sure that they would out gun Starin. But Blackwood's commanding officer was very strict on what could be brought through. Will didn't really understand why that was, until Blackwood asked him if he had ever watched Star Trek. Then the penny dropped. They couldn't have weapons that were significantly more advanced than those already on Vitae. If the folk of Vitae advanced technologically too quickly, they could do irreparable harm to their environment and planet. They needed to learn the lessons of physics before they got ahead of themselves and blew themselves up!! The only reason that Blackwood and his team had been allowed to intervene in the war against Starin was because Starin had already brought Earth technology to Vitae and was using it against folk. Field Marshal Von Schrader needed to close that portal to prevent any further theft of technology and that was the only reason they had intervened.

Finally, the Allied Magiks had everything ready. Blackwood and his team had ensured that all folk understood what they were to do and where they were to go. Rosa had briefed Will and the RDF of their role, and they were ready and waiting. They were to take a rail support vehicle, which consisted of two wagons, equipped with archers, machine guns and magikal attack equipment, behind the Darjeeling and wait for Starin's war train to enter the fray. Will's orders were to disable the War Engine at all costs, and this was the special task that he had alluded to when talking to Steele all those weeks ago.

Humans weren't affected by the red gas which the war train spewed out. It made sense then, that humans be the ones to destroy the engine. Initially, Will hadn't been sure how they would achieve this task but, as the number of human defectors grew, Will and Rosa had come up with a plan. It was a risky one which could lead to them all being killed. But this was war and survival was not guaranteed. All he could do was kiss the kitsune he loved and then take Sherpa to the staging post to await the signal to proceed.

Starin's forces formed up outside the castle and prepared for the battle ahead. The mad king was there, observing the battle. He was clad, from head to toe in magik-repelling armour and was absolutely certain that he was safe from this magikal attack.

General Johnson approached the King and asked for his permission to commence the assault, knowing that Starin would not want to wait for his enemy to make the first move. The King grinned at Johnson and was just about to order the attack when an almighty explosion ripped through the air. Both Johnson and Starin staggered like drunks, trying to stay on their feet. Never before had they felt such a concussion. Starin made a mental note to get Havesh to create more powerful explosives, but that was the last coherent thought he had that night.

The air was full of smoke and falling debris and there was a sound that neither man could identify at first but, as the smoke cleared, they could see that it was the sound of the

Allied Magik army advancing on the walls of Stronghelm. The magik scum had dealt the first blow. The King was apoplectic with rage and ordered the Allied Magik army be ripped apart.

Both armies had been eagerly anticipating this battle, knowing that it could well be the last one - the final battle in a war that had lasted generations. There may not have always been outright fighting between the two factions, but there had always been hostility. Never before had humans and magikal folk fought together, and it was that union that had made the difference this time. The coming of Will Thorpe to Vitae had changed the world forever.

22
OPERATION GRAND SLAM

After the initial explosion, General Ember ordered the tanks forward. In the weeks since the retaking of the City of Hope fifty new tanks had been built. The ones they had used in the previous battle had all failed in one way or another, which had led So'Ren, Francis and Blackwood to come up with some improvements to the next batch. These were stronger, slightly faster and much more agile and manoeuvrable. They were more able to avoid obstacles now and this had been a massive improvement. Many of the previous tanks had broken their tracks by hitting obstacles that had not been seen until the last moment. But the mark 2 tanks were much more resilient.

Tank number 23 was driven by a kitsune called Phillan. He had shown a real talent for getting tanks into the most inaccessible places during training and had quickly been promoted to tank commander. He had a crew of 6 gunners and 3 tank maintenance crew on board and they were probably the most efficient crew in the tank regiment. They had been given the task of shielding the infantry as they made their way towards the castle walls. The infantry were very vulnerable to Starin's 'advanced weaponry' and the tanks were the only things in the Allied Magik armoury that could get close enough to the enemy to destroy that weaponry. Phillan had decided that he was going to destroy more of the enemy weapons than any other tank commander. He had a bet on with the commander of tank 46, a salamander called Sparx, that he would take out at least 4 of the machine gun stations that the scouts had told them were positioned all around the castle walls. Sparx thought he was nuts and that he would probably fall into a ditch before he could even get to the walls! Phillan was happy to prove him wrong, arriving at the walls with all his infantry intact behind him, marching along like duckings following their mother. The soot from the engines on each tank was having the beneficial effect of camouflaging the Allied Magik troops, making it incredibly hard for Starin's troops to see them in the dark of the night and amongst the smoke and debris. This, of course, had been the point of the initial massive explosion that Blackwood had set off.

Following the reports of the Royal Marines after their recon missions, the tank commanders had all been briefed to watch out for small, agile vehicles called Jeeps, which had a weapon mounted on the back. These weapons had the capability of shredding the tanks minimal armour plating and killing the crew inside. Phillan was damn sure that this wasn't going to happen to his crew. As he approached the huge set of wooden gates set into the castle walls, he saw that the concussion of the initial explosion had damaged the locking mechanism and they were slightly ajar. Insidc thc gates was a row of at least 20 Jeeps, waiting to enter the battle. If that happened, they could cause utter devastation to the Allied Magik's tanks. Blackwood's team had only seen 2 of these vehicles and whilst they had known that there could be more, no one had anticipated this many.

Each tank crew had been given a radio which enabled them to communicate with the central command post, manned by Ember, Rosa and Blackwood. They were under strict orders not to use the crystals unless it was urgent as they were unsure whether Starin had the ability to intercept their communication. However, Phillan was fairly sure that this qualified as an emergency so quickly called out to the central command to ask for instructions. Blackwood's calm, authoritative voice came back over the crystal with a very simple command.

"Destroy them! I will send you some support."

Phillan's heart started beating a little faster in his chest.

"Gunner's, make ready to fire," he called back to his crew. They were already prepared, but this was part of the drill and it felt calming to run through the process as they had practised it over the past weeks.

"Ready to fire," came the reply.

Phillan moved 23 forward and into the best possible position to bring his main cannon to bear. All other guns were ready to fire as soon as that first shot had been sent into the gates.

"Fire cannon one!"

"Firing."

It was a direct hit and the gates flew apart in a shower of splinters.

"Fire cannon 2!"

"Firing."

The first jeep in the line left the floor in an almighty fiery ball, flipping over and landing on top of the next jeep in line.

"Hah! Two in one. Great shot boss!" came a voice from the back of the tank.

"Fire at will," Phillan bellowed over the noise of the engine and of the cannons being reloaded. The magikal rapid-fire elemental guns thundered into action and several more of the jeeps were reduced to smoking scrap. But the destruction had brought the attention of the Jeep drivers and they were all powering up their own weapons. Phillan was a sitting mother duck now. He put the tank into reverse to try and get some distance but didn't want to leave any of these jeeps working as he knew the damage they might cause. He quickly looked to his crew and as one, they nodded to him. They knew that this was a suicide mission, but they also knew that this was the only way to save the lives of their friends and loved ones. Phillan threw the tank into forward gear and headed straight for the jeeps; his crew firing all the while, taking out as many as they could. Finally, they ran out of ammunition and there was nothing else they could do. Then Phillan came up with a plan. He aimed the tank at the next jeep in line and revved the engine.

"Boss, what are you doing," one of the crew called?

"Well, you know that we have no ammo left?"

"Yes, we are aware of that. Shouldn't we withdraw," the same crewman asked?

"Where is the fun in that? Let's try to drive right over the top of them."

Phillan looked at his crew questioningly. They returned his look, firstly with fear and disbelief in their eyes. But slowly, seeing his determination the fear changed to acceptance. They nodded and Phillan plunged the tank forward, towards the first jeep in the line. They hit it with a hard jolt and then rocked upwards. Phillan could no longer see the jeeps below him but was sure he was heading in the right direction. They bumped and swayed alarmingly as they moved from vehicle to vehicle, destroying them with the sheer weight of the tank. Just as they were about the reach the last jeep, the tank lurched sideways as its tracks met thin air, rather than the metal of the jeeps roof. Phillan nudged the tank to the left and felt traction again. Releasing the breath he hadn't realised he was holding, Phillan whooped with relief. They had made it. The crazy plan had worked and the whole crew cheered out loud.

"Wow, boss. You are crushing it today," one of the gunners joked.

"Yup, but they are on to us now. Where is that back up?"

All of a sudden, the remaining jeeps were lit up in an orange glow. A ball of fire flew past the tank, narrowly missing hitting its starboard cannon, and a huge black shadow flew across the sky.

"The dragons are here," Phillan shouted with relief. Nothing but a dragon could have been that accurate. When the flash of light had cleared, all that remained of the jeeps and their crews was a twisted pile of smouldering metal.

"Tank 23 you are clear to withdraw. Bloody good job. Well done," Blackwood called over the radio.

Starin watched the destruction of his black wheels with dismay and fury. They had been such a powerful weapon and now, they were destroyed. When he found the person responsible, he would gut them, cut them limb from limb.

His crazed mind took him through all of the most painful punishments he could think of, and he was giggling to himself as he ordered the War Engine to be sent into the battle. He would show these magik scum what happened to those who defied him!

What Starin didn't know was that this was the moment Will was waiting for. The chance to destroy the monster vehicle that Starin had created. Will threw open Sherpa's regulator. The engine charged onto the tracks and headed straight for the War Engine. The Royal Marines and Steele's elite fighters were hanging off the side, providing covering fire. For this mission, Blackwood's second in command, Cpl "Banjo" West, had joined the party. He was the demolitions expert in the squad and what he didn't know about causing explosions wasn't worth knowing. This wasn't going to be a stealth attack, even with all of the noise of the battle going on around them, Sherpa was a noisy little engine, and it wasn't long before one of the War Engine's gunners noticed the engine approaching on the adjacent line. He aimed his gas nozzle at Sherpa and its crew and fired. As Sherpa grew closer, they could see the grin on the gunner's face, but the joke was on him as there were no magik-users to be affected by the gas. Only very, very ticked off humans who were all excellent shots with their machine guns!

Will handed the controls of the engine over to one of the other drivers and prepared to leap from the cab. He was not looking forward to this manoeuvre and had tried to dissuade Banjo and Steele from adopting the crazy plan, but it was the only solution they could think of. So there he was hanging off the cab, waiting for the perfect moment to jump onto the war engine, with Banjo and Steele beside him.

"Steady, steady. Go", Banjo shouted. Steele and Banjo made the jump into the rear wagon look effortless, but Will caught his foot on the lip of the door and face-planted at their feet in a snotty heap.

"Not a word. Not one word!" he warned them as he held his sore nose.

The two were so busy trying not to laugh that they couldn't speak right at that moment, but Will knew that he wasn't safe from their mick taking for long.

Originally, Blackwood had wanted to blow the gas canister, and the train to kingdom come, but the risk of the gas spreading towards the magik-users was too great and they had quickly decided that there had to be another way. Will had suggested that, as the approach to Stronghelm was on a fairly steep gradient, they should just detach the wagons, with the explosives on board and allow them to detonate at a safe distance. The Allied Magiks had been told to avoid the foot of the hill at all costs.

Now, Will, Banjo and Steele just had to fight their way to the front wagon, laying explosives as they went, disconnect the wagons and hope that they didn't get blown up in the process. They also had to do all of this in a very short timescale. Fortunately, the tight space within the wagons meant that even Will managed to hit whomever he was aiming at and most of the troops inside the wagons were unaware that Will and his team were onboard until it was too late.

Every time they passed a red gas tank, Banjo set an explosive device. He could have them in place and ready to blow before Will had even managed to catch his breath and it wasn't long before they had reached the very front wagon.

Will was just about to pull the pin which held the coupler in place when General Watkins leapt into the wagon. Where he came from, no-one knew but Steele reacted in an instant.

"Go! Do what you need to do. I've got this," and he charged at the General with the fury of a man possessed. Steele hated Watkins with a passion. He was the commander of Starin's forces in the field and a wicked, evil man who enjoyed inflicting pain on others. Steele knew that it was Watkins who had come up with the ideas for the concentration camps and he would never forgive the man for treating Ebunnie's folk in that way.

Will and Banjo knew that they had to let Steele deal with the General. There wasn't time to debate it; they had a mission to complete. Will reached for the pin and pulled it, then lifted the isolating valves on both the engine and wagon which allowed the wagons to roll safely away whilst the engine continued forwards. Next, Will and Banjo had to take care of the engine driver and fireman which Banjo seemed to thoroughly enjoy. Blackwood had said he was a brawler and Will could see why. A swift uppercut to the jaw of the driver and an elbow into the stomach of the Fireman, followed by Will and his trusty fire shovel manoeuvre and the crew were taken care of. They brought the engine to a safe stop and leapt down. The wagons had continued after the engine for a moment, until gravity did its thing and started them moving down the incline.

"Steele! It's time to go" Will shouted.

"Coming, dear," came the joking reply. Steele slammed his fist into the side of Watkin's head and the General fell like a sack of potatoes. Steele leapt from the wagon, landing in a heap on the side of the tracks. Will gave him a look that seemed to say "I won't tell, if you don't" and Banjo pressed the detonator. The three friends turned and walked up the hill, looking for all the world like 3 cowboys who had just killed the bad guy! As the explosion lit up the sky, Will put his arms on the shoulders of Banjo and Steele and said,

"Well, that was a blast."

"No. Just, No," Banjo muttered.

Once the dust had cleared, Will looked over at the Allied Magiks' forces. They were now within the castle walls and there was little resistance left in Starin's troops. Will could feel Rosa through their heart bond, but it didn't stop him worrying about her and hoping that she was OK.

Rosa was, at that moment, cutting her way through a seemingly endless mob of human soldiers. Her fellow Allied Magiks were struggling to keep up with her and, had they been in competition with her, they would most certainly have been losing. Many fell at the hands of the humans and it was all Rosa could do to ignore their screams of agony. Rosa's sword, Firebringer, could cut through almost anything that she encountered at the best of times, but when it was also charged with elemental magik and being wielded by the kitsune, it was practically unstoppable, and the human troops didn't stand a chance. Rosa was clearly enjoying herself; she was in the castle of Starin, her most hated enemy, avenging the death of Nirvana, her father who had died at the hands of humans many years earlier and of so many other members of the folk who had been killed.

Enemy after enemy fell to Firebringer and as Rosa and her troops made their way deeper and deeper into the castle they found even more evidence of the atrocities committed by Starin and his predecessors. There were minotaurs' heads, mounted on plinths, valuable artefacts in glass cases that had been removed from temples of folk and the embalmed body of a dwarf, nailed to a piece of wood. There were others, but Rosa was moving quickly through the castle and didn't stop to examine them all.

After what seemed like hours, Rosa and her team arrived at a junction packed with human soldiers. They were arranged in rows and completely filled the corridor ahead.

"What are you going to do now, magik scum?" a human with gold on his shoulders asked. "Did you think you could actually defeat us?" He threw back his head and laughed as if he had cracked the funniest joke ever. That was until he coughed a spray of blood out and collapsed to the floor.

"Don't you know that that is not the way to address a lady?" Owen Trelisker asked, just before jumping into action and attacking the soldiers blocking the corridor. Owen hadn't come alone either. He had half of his unit of elite fighters had emerged from a connecting corridor, without making a sound. Rosa and her team re-joined the fight, and the humans were very quickly overwhelmed by their sheer skill. They knew that Starin's study was nearby, and they had to reach it if they were to capture him alive.

During Owen's time as a spy, he had made it his mission to learn every twist and turn of the castle. He headed off down a corridor and called Rosa to follow him. The castle was like a maze, but Owen guided them straight to the doors of Starin's study which were locked shut. But what was a lock when you had access to elemental magik? It wasn't long before the door was in splinters and Rosa and Owen were looking at an empty room. Starin wasn't there, but he had left Rosa a note.

"You took everything from me. Now I shall take everything from you."

Rosa knew exactly who Starin was referring to and her eyes widened in terror. She looked straight at Owen and he knew what she needed to do just as well as she did.

"Go," he told her.

Rosa shifted into her fox form and charged back out of the study. She had to get to Will. Time slowed as she tore through the castle. As she ran, her mind kept playing her mother's death, but this time it was Will who was being run through by Starin's sword. Will, who couldn't defend himself unless he thought Rosa was in danger. Will, who was the only thing that she had to live for. Will, her beloved! The images got worse and worse as she ran, despite the fact that she could feel him through the bond that they shared. She knew exactly where he was and skidded into the courtyard where the Darjeeling was sitting. Will was helping the medicas to deal with the huge numbers of injured soldiers, from both sides, and had no idea that he was in imminent danger. Just behind him, creeping along the side of the engine, was Starin. He had his sword drawn and it was raised above his head, ready to take the killing blow.

Rosa absorbed the scene in an instant. She charged at Starin, crashing into him and knocking him off balance. The pain that shot through her as Rosa changed back into her bipedal form was incredible. For a moment, she couldn't move. But that only lasted a second. Will was in danger, and pain would not stop her from protecting him. She drew Firebringer and charged into battle with the crazed king.

Will had felt Rosa coming into the courtyard through the

bond, he felt her terror and whirled around just in time to see her collide into Starin who was clad in a complete suit of armour of anti magik armour. As she changed out of her fox form, she took a moment to look back at Will and he smiled and nodded at her.

Fighting Starin, without touching his armour was no mean feat, but that wasn't going to stop Rosa. Will did his best to keep Starin's guard off Rosa. With his anelacce in hand he attacked the humans with all of the skill and knowledge that the warrior bond gave him. Seeing his beloved in such peril was enough to activate the bond and Will let it happen. He gave in to it completely and became a fighting machine. He knew it was the only way that he could help Rosa in her battle with Starin. In years to come, legends would grow up around this battle; one human against an army. Will wasn't alone though. Owen and his troops arrived to back Will up and the guards were quickly subdued. Now, it was down to Rosa.

The fight was intense and both were injured, with dozens of small cuts and stab wounds. Starin was a good fighter, but he was much heavier and not of sound mind! There was only so long that he could use brute strength against the speed and grace of Rosa. At first he managed to get a few glancing blows in and Rosa had cuts in both her arms. But his dominance didn't last long. Each flash of her katana sapped a little more of Starin's strength. She danced away from his heavier blade and he was no match for her momentum. Each time the elementally charged blade cut through his enhanced armour, he lost a little more blood until he had nothing left.Finally, Rosa had him down on the floor with Firebringer held to his throat. Both were smeared with blood and panting from the exertion, but Starin was barely able to hold himself up at that moment. Rosa stood straight and proud, having avenged the deaths of her parents, knowing that she had taken everything from Starin. His kingdom, his son and his strength.

Seeing Starin on the ground was the final straw for the remainder of the human army and the Allied Magiks were left looking at each other in wonder. Had they actually done it? Had they won the war? As they realised that they had indeed won, a cheer broke out and it rippled throughout the castle. But no-one had told Starin that he had lost. Taking advantage of the distraction, Starin leapt to his feet and ran from the courtyard. Out of the corner of his eye he could see General Johnson beckoning to him and just behind him was the Baldwin locomotive, which still had steam coming from its chimney. By the time Starin had raced over to the engine, Johnson was on board and holding his hand out to pull him into the cab. How Starin had managed to get all the way to the engine was a mystery. He was injured from his fight with Rosa and limping quite heavily, but it didn't slow him down enough for anyone to catch up with him.

Once in the cab, Starin saw that Havesh had also managed to make it onto the war train and it was Havesh who was driving the engine out of Stronghelm. Havesh was an excellent, if completely insane, engineer and he knew exactly how the engine worked. But there is a big difference between knowing how the engine worked and actually working it. Despite Johnson yelling at Havesh for more speed, he could not make the engine move any more quickly. He needed help to shovel coal into the fire, but Starin was the king and therefore above such menial tasks, and Johnson was a general. He gave orders, he did not carry them out. This meant that Havesh was shovelling coal and trying to drive the engine at the same time.

"One of you is going to have to drive. I can't do both jobs," Havesh gasped out. He wasn't used to hard labour and shovelling coal is not an easy job.

Johnson had no idea how to drive an engine and Starin only had a vague clue. But in the end the mad king took hold of the regulator and tried his best to keep the engine going at top speed.

After the initial shock of Starin's escape from the courtyard, Will had charged to the Darjeeling, shouting for it to be uncoupled from its carriages. Rosa quickly followed and they both leapt into the cab. Will instructed Rosa to build up the heat in the infernoss crystal and to keep it hot. Rosa poured her elemental magic into the crystal and it rapidly began to create steam in the boiler. Usually, this wouldn't be necessary as the infernoss crystal could heat the water in the boiler with a simple instruction, but they were in a hurry and the engine needed to be moving quickly if they were to catch Starin. Once the carriages were uncoupled, Will released the brakes, opened the regulator and charged out of Stronghelm, determined to catch Starin and make him pay for the harm he had caused.

23
THE GREAT CHASE

The silence of the forest outside of Stronghelm was shattered as the two engines raced down the tracks. Neither the tracks, nor the engines were built for this kind of punishment but both drivers were desperate. Starin to escape and Will to prevent that from happening again.

Despite the Darjeeling being a much less powerful engine than the Baldwin, it was much lighter, and it had caught the Baldwin and was following right behind. Having Will and Rosa working as a team had meant that Starin had no chance of outrunning them and as the ground started rising up a steep incline, Will knew he had them. Rosa climbed out of the cab and started inching along the side of Sherpa. It was hot so close to the boiler and there were a lot of moving parts but, somehow, Rosa managed to leap onto the front running plate of the Darjeeling and balance there. The plan was simple enough. Bring the Darjeeling up to the buffers of the Baldwin, couple the engines together and then Will could start to bring both engines to a halt. In the meantime, Rosa would deal with the king.

Carefully, Will edged Sherpa closer and closer until there

was a clang. Havesh realised what was going on and told Starin to open the regulator to maximum, but it was too late. Rosa had acted with lightning speed and the coupling hooks were already in place, locking the two engines together. At Rosa's signal, Will began applying the brakes, slowly at first but then with more and more pressure. Then he added in the reverse gear. Sparks and steam flew from the little engine as it gave everything it had to stop the two engines. But it wasn't enough. The Baldwin continued to gain speed. Will applied maximum braking and the brakes were glowing red hot. When Will whistled to warn Rosa that the brakes weren't going to last much longer, she was already moving. She had been able to smell the burning and had thrown herself onto the Baldwin's tender and drawn her sword. General Johnson moved to intercept the approaching kitsune, but he was no match for her skill. Before long both Johnson and Havesh had involuntarily vacated the Baldwin and were laying in a snotty heap on the ground next to the tracks.

Will blasted the whistle in celebration and Rosa grinned back at him. Then she turned to face her real foe.

Starin climbed onto the tender and joined Rosa. They both knew that this was the final battle and that it would likely be to the death.

"You can yield to me now. You were too weak to save Nirvana, you are too weak to defeat me," Starin taunted Rosa. He was trying to make her fly into a rage and become reckless. He knew it was the only way that he could defeat her. Rosa rose to the bait and ethereal flames started to dance all over her body and down the blade of Firebringer. Her eyes blazed red and she struck. However, Starin had made a mistakc. Rosa did get mad, but she didn't get reckless. She had been taught to fight by Nirvana and had spent her youth perpetually angry. Anger made her more controlled, not less.

The engines were still flying down the track and the coal in the tender was unstable. Rosa caught her foot and fell to the floor, leaving herself open to Starin's attack. He raised his sword above his head and drove it down towards Rosa's chest. Will saw this unfolding and slammed the brakes on as hard as he could. Both engines lurched and Starin's blow went wide hitting Rosa in the shoulder, but with a glancing blow rather that with full force. In that instant, Rosa had her chance and she took it. She raised Firebringer and slashed at Starin's sword hand. The sword, and the hand fell to the ground and Starin screamed in pain and anguish. There was no time for celebration though. Rosa clambered down to the cab of the Baldwin and applied the brakes, slowing and finally, stopping both engines in a cloud of steam and the sound of both whistles being blasted in relief.

Will and Rosa leapt from their engines and ran to each other. They held each other close, both crying tears of joy. The war was over. But Starin wasn't dead and he made one last attempt to kill his enemy. Out of the corner of his eye, Will saw Starin run at them with what looked like a dagger aimed at Rosa. He snatched up Vengence, aimed and fired, all in the blink of an eye. The warrior bond gave him the speed he needed to protect his beloved, but not necessarily the aim he would have liked. The bullet struck Starin, but not in the gut which is where Will was aiming. It entered the King's body a little lower than that, but Will was just relieved that it hit him at all.

It was a killing blow and the mad King fell to the floor with an agonised, and slightly surprised, look on his face.

Rosa and Will took a moment to enjoy standing in the peaceful forest before throwing Starin's body onto the roof of the Baldwin's cab and tying it there, ready for the journey back to Stronghelm.

Will tried to get to Steele before he could see his father's body but the young Prince was waiting at the gate for them.

"I'm sorry Steele, I should have covered him up. You shouldn't have to see your father like that."

"It's OK, Will. He stopped being my father many years ago. But... I have to ask. Did you intend to shoot him... well... there? I mean, I know he was a pri…"

"No! No I did not! I was aiming at his gut and, well we all know that I am not the best shot and no... no... definitely not. No man would deliberately hit another man in the... well... you know." Will had blushed his usual bright red and Rosa was, once again, laughing at his embarrassment.

The three friends were joined by Ebunnie and So'Ren and they all walked into Stronghelm together, laughing and smiling. The war was over, and they could live in peace.

EPILOGUE
AFTERMATH

Three months had passed since the defeat of Starin, and peace reigned for the most part. The human generals had either surrendered or been captured and prosecuted for their part in the destruction and torture of the Folk of Vitae. Their punishments had been decided by the new king and the Vitaen Parliament, which was made up of representatives from both human and folk kind. Steele had been very reluctant to take the crown but, despite their experience of Steele's predecessors, the humans had wanted him. They had seen his actions and they knew that he was not his father. He was his own man and would make a great king. So, Steele had married Ebunnie and been crowned king on the same day. The celebrations had gone on for days and there were more than a few sore heads around.

Rosa had called for a vote for the leadership of the folk and she had been elected unanimously, much to her surprise. She did not lead the parliament, but she was one of its key advisors. She had advised that the railway network be rebuilt and reinforced, and it had become critical to the rebuilding of Vitae. Getting folk and supplies to all corners of the realm would be vital if they were to bring in a harvest and ensure that folk didn't starve that winter. Many had been displaced by the war and crops had not been tended as they should have been. It took a lot of combined effort from farmers and magik-users alike to ensure there was enough food for the coming winter and even then, it would be a tough year ahead. This rebuilding of the railway had kept Will very busy and he had not spent as much time with Rosa as they would both have liked. But, after 3 months, things had started to settle down and the two young lovers were enjoying their new lives together.

Blackwood and his Royal Marines had spent a few weeks helping with the rebuilding but had soon been called back to their world to help search for some missing princesses. They had promised to return over the next few months and help as and when they could, and they had. During these visits the subject of the engines had come up and Will had insisted that three of the engines should go back to the Ginger Line. He knew how tough they would have been finding things without the Garratt and Number 4 to do the heavy work. The Alco would also, eventually be returned to the Ginger Line but it was needed for the work on Vitae for a short while. The Darjeeling was his and it would remain on Vitae with him.

Will had been told that all fire crystals and Vitean technology would have to be removed from the engines that were leaving and this had saddened him. He knew how hard, and expensive it was to keep a line running and coal was only going to get more expensive as time went on. But, So'Ren had a sneaky idea and so, early one morning he had called Will to the engine sheds and they hadn't emerged again for several days. Only Rosa was allowed in with food for them.

So'Ren and Will knew that Blackwood would be searching for crystals and would know if they hadn't been removed. But he would be looking for whole crystals in the firebox. So'Ren and Will found a way to add crushed crystals to the walls of the fireboxes of the three engines in such a way that they would be invisible unless you knew they were there, and even then, you could only find them by feeling along the walls. For years, the accountants on the Ginger Line couldn't understand why they were using so little coal and after the few staff who knew about the crystals had retired or moved on, the mystery was forgotten and the engines were just thought to be very efficient.

So'Ren's designs for the new Vitaen engines were quickly put into action and he became well known for the amazing machines that he created. With the added bonus of magik, the engines were built in record time and put to use before the summer was over. Until then, the Vitaens had managed with the Darjeeling and refurbished Baldwin after the Alco had finally been returned. Rosa made So'Ren the Minister for Science and Technology and he continued to make amazing machines for many years to come.

Sgt Blackwood came to see Will just before returning through the portal one day.

"Will, the next time I come through will be the last. You don't need us here anymore and we have stayed longer than was strictly necessary. I need to be sure that you want to remain on Vitae. We will likely not be permitted back after we leave next time. Don't answer me now. Take some time to think about it. Tell me when I get back."

Will already knew that he wanted to stay. He missed his

friends on Earth, but he loved his life on Vitae. He had never had the sense of purpose that he had here before. He loved Rosa with every fibre of his body and couldn't imagine life without her now. No, he was home, and he would never leave Vitae.

Blackwood had known that already, but he liked Will and had wanted to give him the option to return one last time. Blackwood had come to love Vitae too and wondered whether he would be allowed to retire there one day. He would have to speak to the field marshal about it. So, when Blackwood returned, he asked Will one more time, already knowing what his response would be. When Will refused Blackwood nodded and then handed Will two packages. He shook the young man's hand and then pulled him into a brief hug.

"Be well, Will. I hope our paths cross again one day." And with that, he was gone.

Will walked over to Rosa with a grin on his face.

"I have something for you, love" he told her and then beckoned her over to the engine shed where the first of So'Ren's engines was being steamed up for it's first outing.

Rosa opened the package and found two name plates. One had the name "Nirvana" written in English, the other written in Bengali.

"We thought we would name this engine after your mum, would that be alright?" he asked.

"She would have loved that. Thank you Will." Rosa said through tears, as she placed the first name plate in its bracket next to the cab of the engine.

"There is something else I wanted to ask, and I guess it is fitting that Nirvana is here. How do folk ask their beloved to marry them? I mean, there is this foxy lady that I would love to marry, but I want to ask her properly. On my world, we get down on one knee, like this, and we offer a ring, like this one here, and we ask if the person we love would marry us."

So'Ren and half the RDF were all stood with their mouths open, watching Will get down on one knee and offer a small, square box to Rosa. Inside the box was a stunning green ring, the colour of Rosa's eyes. Rosa, for her part, was standing with her eyes as large as saucers, staring at the beautiful ring and at her beloved kneeling in the oil and metal shavings that had yet to be swept up.

She gathered herself and then asked,

"So, on your world, if the foxy lady wanted to say yes, how would she do it? Would she accept the ring, oh just like that, yes!" Rosa didn't get any further as Will pushed the ring onto her finger and then kissed her soundly, much to the delight of everyone in the engine sheds that day.

On Vitae, a marriage is called "Heartbonding" and the ceremony took place in Rosa's garden. During the beautiful ceremony Will felt a prickling on the back of his neck and was sure that someone was watching them. He turned his head and saw the faint form of Nirvana's spirit at the edge of the garden. She gave Will a nod of approval, smiled at her daughter and then disappeared, never to be seen on Vitae again.

Will turned to Rosa, who had seen her mother, and smiled at her. Whatever the future held, Will knew that the two of them would face it together.